D0105052

Lava

By Pamela Ball

A NOVEL

LAVA

W. W. Norton & Company

New York   London

Part of this novel appeared in *Fiction South/Fiction North,*
published by Ridgefield Press

For information about permission to reproduce selections from this book,
write to Permissions, W. W. Norton & Company, Inc. 500 Fifth Avenue,
New York, N.Y. 10110.

The text of this book is composed in Monotype Walbaum with the display
set in Lithos Black. Composition and manufacturing by The Maple-Vail
Book Manufacturing Group.
Book design by Charlotte Staub

Library of Congress Cataloging-in-Publication Data

Ball, Pamela.
Lava : a novel / by Pamela Ball.
p.   cm.
ISBN 0-393-04024-0
I. Title.
PS3552.A4554L38   1997
813'.54—dc20   96-31660
                                          CIP

W. W. Norton & Company, Inc., 500 Fifth Avenue, New York, N.Y. 10110
http://www.wwnorton.com

W. W. Norton & Company Ltd., 10 Coptic Street, London WC1A 1PU
1 2 3 4 5 6 7 8 9 0

In memory of Jerry Stern
and for
Lulu Caruso Ball

Lava

For her support and thoughtful criticism during
the writing of this book I'd like to thank
my very good friend Pat MacEnulty

As well, I'd like to thank Taylor and Georgia,
and especially Carol Houck Smith.

*F*or her support and thoughtful criticism during
the writing of this book I'd like to thank
my very good friend Pat MacEnulty

As well, I'd like to thank Taylor and Georgia,
and especially Carol Houck Smith.

Lava

What if you lived in a world where you could wake the dead, where men had a shark jaw buried in their backs just as the shark god did when he stepped on shore and became human? A place where scalding lava ran through the streets of the town and down into the hissing sea. Where women picked up guns and never put them down again, where it rained three days out of three, and ghosts drank from the rain gutters and huddled under the eaves of the wooden buildings. What if you lived in a town like that? It would still just be Hilo.

1

*I*n Hilo, the dead sharks were hung on hooks under the rafters of the small wooden buildings. As days passed the line of gray flesh multiplied, and when no one was looking, I put my hands out and touched the hard, roughened skin. The blood pooled on the ground and the fishermen gathered in circles around the edges of the blood and later their slippers left tracks down the sidewalk, mixing the blood of one dead shark with another. The fishing supply store ran out of gaffs and marlin hooks and rope, and the shoe store ran out of the high wooden getas that would keep our feet away from the blood. It was like nothing I'd ever seen.

There was a line of sharks and a crowd of people milling around with tape measures flashing in their hands. The shark bounty had the shape of a celebration, if you stood far enough away. If you stood far enough away, almost anything would take a shape. Even after five years, Ivan was still the cause of everything around me, what I saw and what I felt. I couldn't tell if I was more possessed by his absence than by the man himself.

Absence is a strange thing. I couldn't say that I loved this man more the longer he was away from me. And yet, I didn't love him less. When a man took himself out of your life, you could do what you wanted to with him. I blamed him, that was central to everything, the one part that couldn't be overlooked.

The dead sharks were hanging on hooks, and the flies came and quickly darkened the edges of the eyes, the mouth, so that from a distance the sharks looked like they were almost smiling, a black, rotting smile.

The shark bounty was due to the boy. I couldn't get used to the idea of the boy, never mind that he wasn't a boy, really, but a young man named Nicholas, Ivan's stepson.

A week earlier, Nicholas had arrived on the Big Island, and had called me up. I told him where I lived and he drove a rental car up the mountain from Hilo to the house I'd lived in all my life—before I knew Ivan, with Ivan, and since Ivan had left me for this boy's mother.

Nicholas was proud of the fact that he'd found me, prouder still that he had a fake ID, a driver's license making him old enough to rent a car.

I didn't point out that anyone could have found me, I'd been in one place my whole life. I wasn't the one who'd left.

Nicholas wore the long gangly limbs of a boy racing to catch up to the man. He seemed so amazed to be on the Big Island that I had the feeling I was living at the end of the world. For a boy coming from the middle of the Mainland, perhaps Hawaii truly was the end of the world.

He showed me his driver's license, and in the photo he looked even younger, about eleven. He said he could get me one, too.

"I could probably shave a few years off," I said.

"No," he said, "not that. A whole new identity."

He was dressed in safari clothes, the clothes of a traveler. That was when I gave in entirely, seeing him as a mother might, a young boy adjusting his man-sized belt, bunching up his long pants. He was in the costume of an explorer, a discoverer who thought he'd made it to the end of the world, and hadn't yet figured out that the end of the world kept running away from you.

I asked how Ivan was, and he shrugged.

"We're not getting along so hot."

I nodded as if I understood what he meant. Perhaps it wasn't much at all, something as simple as bad grades. At least he was talking, and I didn't want to start asking questions that would shut him up.

"You want to help me get that potting soil inside before it starts raining?" I asked, nodding towards the greenhouses and the bags of soil stacked up against one of them.

We walked across the lawn to the first greenhouse, and as I opened the door, he stepped in after me.

The protea were at the front, each plant topped with a flame-colored bloom. Behind them were rows of saplings I'd just transplanted, and the back half of the greenhouse was full of orchids. A thousand blooming plants I needed to sell in a hurry.

"Wow," he said, looking around.

"Yeah, I love it in here," I said, clearing a place for the bags of soil. "It's kind of like a sanctuary. Sometimes it's hard to leave."

Nicholas walked between the rows of blooming orchids, and his hand hovered like a bee, hesitating over the flowers.

"It looks like a high school prom," Nicholas said, smiling, his hand still moving over the orchids.

We stacked the bags of soil, and he quickly became tired, though he tried not to show it.

He talked as we worked and I was surprised at

what he already knew about the Big Island. It sounded like Ivan had told him everything he knew, and I could only think that to describe a place so thoroughly was to miss it deeply. Nicholas wanted to see everything, the beaches of black sand, the fields of wetland taro, the coastline, the lava flows. Ivan had even told him about the auction at the fish market, where clusters of men called out prices and slid the frozen ahis across the wet floors, the tongues of the fish round and hard as broomsticks. He asked if we could watch for Pele, the goddess of the volcanos.

"How long will you be here?" I asked.

He shrugged. "I sort of dropped out of school," he said.

"Ah," I said.

"It's like my mother and Ivan have this whole future planned out for me, you know? It's kind of getting to me. So I thought of doing something different."

"Well, I'm sure it will all still be there if you change your mind," I offered, handing him the final bag of soil.

"Maybe," he said, placing the bag carefully at the top of the stack.

I thought of something. "How are you fixed for money?" I asked.

"I could use a job, I guess," he answered, sounding nervous and unsure.

They didn't give him any money, I thought. A

kid who's come halfway around the world without any money. "Listen," I said, "I've got a little cottage down at the bottom of the hill. More of a shack, really. But if you want to stay there a couple of nights, that'd be okay."

"That'd be great," he said, relief showing in his face.

"It's pretty run-down, but at least it's got electricity."

We went into the house and he called the hotel and canceled his room. I gathered up some sheets and blankets and rubber zoris and we walked down to the cottage.

I handed him the zoris. "One set to wear, the other to slap the roaches," I explained, and left him to settle in.

Later, he came up to the house and into the living room and said he wanted to show me something. He carefully rolled up his sleeve, then turned sideways and held his arm out. There was a tattoo across his pale skin. A boat on the high seas.

Not just any boat, but a clipper ship under full sail and riggings, and another tattoo of a wide anchor that hung below the boat like a crooked smile. I couldn't take my eyes off it.

"There's room for a name here," he said, running his finger across the curve of the anchor.

"A name?"

"I'm supposed to put a name across the anchor when I fall in love."

I didn't say anything. I touched his tattoo and felt his flesh jump under my fingers.

He looked out the window.

I got up out of my chair and stood beside him.

The tattoo made me feel different, restless, like I could put my fist right through the glass and pull it back in again without a mark on me.

What is happening to me, I wondered. And then in the long grass outside, I thought for a moment I saw a fish with a spreading fin, a flash of color as it leapt up away from its predator, twisted in the air, and held there for a moment. I blinked and turned away from the window.

It made me nervous to find Nicholas so large, so fully grown, and I was jealous that he'd spent the last five years with Ivan. Jealous of a boy I liked. It was pitiful, it was beneath me, it was exactly what I felt.

He would have been much easier to deal with in some smaller, less-finished form, not this discoverer parting the large leaves of the past, in some jungle movie of his own making.

Nicholas wanted to work on a fishing boat, so the next morning I drove him down the mountain to the harbor in Hilo. We rode in my old Ford truck that had to be left running or kickstarted, and I sat in the cab with the engine idling, pointing out different boats that I knew were hiring.

It was early in the morning, and the flat side of

the mountain behind us was a soft pink, the same color that was reflected on the water, and a moment later the water had turned metal-colored, the rain started, and Nicholas was scampering from boat to boat, the wings of his bones showing through his wet shirt. The first boat probably would have hired him, except for the oddness of his clothing. I could have gone down onto the dock myself, introduced him, and gotten him on that first boat, but I had the feeling it wasn't what he wanted.

Soon enough, he'd found a boat that would hire him, and turned to wave at me in the truck. He looked like a giant windmill, his long arms pumping away with a certain sweet eagerness, and I realized that he wasn't going to quit waving until I waved back, so I opened the door of the truck and stood on the running board and waved back with the same wide loopy motions.

The last time I looked, he was halfway out the harbor in a flag-line boat, wearing his hat cocked to one side and securely fastened under his chin, the whole world out there in front of him, the way it always is for a boy that age, in a boat.

After Nicholas's fishing boat rounded the breakwater, I jumped off the running board and twisted my hair into a long rope, then up into a loose bun, and anchored it with a chopstick. Ivan had liked to pull the chopstick from my hair and watch it unwind, the way a rope falling overboard follows an anchor, slowly at first and then picking up speed until the rope itself blurs as the weight increases.

The first time I made love with Ivan it was in the greenhouse. It was evening, but I was still working, and he stood to the side and watched me finish air-layering gardenia plants, and he knew perfectly well that we would make love there, just as I did, though we both pretended otherwise.

When I set down the final plant and wiped my hands on a cloth, he came and kissed me, pushing my body back against the long worktable until we slid down beneath it.

We undressed each other, crawling out of our clothes, and our bodies turned green on the floor where the moss and small ferns pushed up through the cracks in the damp concrete, scratching our skin. The moss rubbed into Ivan's black hair and left green streaks across his chest, and he looked like a strange plant hovering over me and I laughed and then he did something unexpected, something wonderful, and I quit laughing.

At the harbor, I gave myself a look in the side mirror, got back into the truck, and drove up to Volcano.

It was five years earlier that Ivan left me for Nicholas's mother, a woman who needed rescuing from a stalled elevator in the hotel where Ivan was in charge of all maintenance and emergencies. Even

I could see the humor in that. We never love anyone as much as someone needing rescue.

Victoria had come to the Big Island as a tourist and was staying in the hotel down on the coast. She had money, and while it wasn't the deciding factor with Ivan, it didn't hurt. Money is a kind of sandpaper, it smooths down the sharp edges, it takes away the surface roughness. Ivan must have liked the idea of being paid to walk away from one life and start another. Who isn't secretly in love with that notion? There had been days when he'd come home and look around, dazed, as if he'd walked into the wrong house, into the wrong life. He was ripe for change and change offered itself.

The afternoon that Nicholas's mother went into the elevator of the hotel and got stuck between floors, Ivan was notified immediately on his emergency beeper. I couldn't ever hear one of those things going off without having the feeling that someone's life was getting ready to change completely.

After the rescue, I found out that Ivan had stayed and talked to the woman while the elevator was being repaired. I asked him what he'd said to keep her from panicking.

He shrugged. "The usual things," he said. " 'You'll be fine.' "

"What else?"

" 'We're doing everything we can.' I think I also

said to just hang on. It doesn't matter what you say, really. The trick is just to say it slowly, give them one word at a time."

He was the first person she saw after the hours it took to fix the elevator, and she must have seen the same things I'd always seen. For me, Ivan was a reward with his black hair the color of split-open coal, and long boat-shaped eyes that went from brown to gold. To me, he was the center of atten- tion. The centipede of attraction, I used to call him. You can wait a whole lifetime to feel its bite.

More than that, it was the sound of his voice. His voice was cool water poured into a cup.

Still, I liked to think of Nicholas's mother as some kind of gosling, hatching after her hours in the elevator, and following forever the first face she saw.

I could think that about her because I'd done the same thing myself. I had recognized Ivan so imme- diately, so completely, I felt that he was something that had been ripped from me without my knowing it, he was what had been missing in me.

I wasn't sure anyone could stand back from a feeling that powerful. If I stood back, I realized that no other person could possibly provide you with yourself, to think so was slightly deranged. But I never stood that far back. Even as a child when the volcano erupted, I knew the place to be was in the middle of the fire, the center of the eruption.

2

---

*W*hat I knew about sharks: There were always more of them around than you thought and for the most part they avoided humans, whether through fear or lack of interest. The first touch was always a surprise, an unexpected toughness to their skin. Sharks had no predators other than themselves, and perhaps they thought they owned the sea, the way humans thought they owned the land. When sharks fought, they rolled their eyes up to protect themselves.

And Ivan? Like a shark, he kept his distance from

most people. His movements were bold, and unexpected. He was always first to dive off the high
cliffs, to go out to sea during storms. I thought he
was trying to find a danger that would match his
own. There were those who never recovered from
the combination of his black hair, gold eyes, and
aloof manner. There were times I thought Ivan
himself hadn't recovered. On the inside of his arms
the skin was soft, but elsewhere it was rough, like a
child's roughened knees. During an orgasm, his eyes
rolled up, slits of white stared out, and he saw nothing at all.

The Hawaiian shark-men came on land in the
form of men, but with one difference, they had a
shark jaw buried in their backs. Their appetites
were still those of a shark, appetites that couldn't be
hidden for long, just as the jaws in their backs
couldn't remain a secret, even though they covered
themselves with cloaks, wound tapa fabric round
their bodies, and went out only after dusk to avoid
the curiosity of others in the same village.

What of their loneliness, their passion? These
topics weren't spoken of when I was a child listening to older people telling the stories of the
shark-men as a way to keep us children in the
neighborhood, to make us wary of strangers, cau-
tious about swimming alone.

I wondered about the shark-men's confusion at

being born of women but with an insatiable longing to cannibalize that same flesh. The transition from one world to another is never complete, there's always some part of our past that is dragged kicking into the present, some story that should have remained hidden.

3

*T*he day after her ordeal in the elevator, Victoria had our unlisted phone number. For all I knew, Ivan had given it to her while she was still stuck. At first she called to say how important it was to be able to reach the one person who knew what she'd been going through in that small black space, and Ivan would roll his eyes at me during their conversations.

When he'd get off the phone we'd laugh about the possibility of a reward, since she was so rich. As we sat in the kitchen late at night, we spent her money on our lives, planned a new lanai to replace the rotted one on the front of our cottage, another greenhouse for my business, more camera equipment for Ivan.

When she called, I'd hand the phone to Ivan and leave the room. But when the calls didn't stop and Ivan no longer rolled his eyes at whatever she was saying, and his voice dropped down to a whisper, she must have heard the palm of his hand pushing across the screens, because she postponed her trip back to the Mainland and had her nanny come out to take care of her young son, Nicholas. By that time, there wasn't all that much to laugh about anymore.

When I thought about it later, wondering at the ease with which Ivan let himself be taken away from me, I thought perhaps it was because she needed him. For some men, that was the most gratifying thing of all, to be needed.

Is that how we reward ourselves for experiencing so much pain, by keeping a bit of that pain running through the bloodstream, the way people who are allergic are given a little bit of the venom in order to save themselves?

On the day Ivan moved to the Mainland with Victoria, all the waterfalls turned upside down, the water rushing straight up the cliffs towards the sky. There were reports of earthquakes around the world, which always meant tidal waves for us. People huddled around their radios and the kona winds blew backwards through all our houses.

Mentally, everyone packed up and evacuated, even though physically they stayed where they were, listening to the transistor radios after the electricity went down. Neighbors who hadn't seen each other in years borrowed hibachis, barbecued together, told stories in the light from hurricane lamps while the children ran through the darkness playing hide and seek in their pajamas, stopping only long enough to get an adult another beer out of the ice chest, or eat a bite of the huge amounts of food that had to be cooked before it spoiled. Growing up in Hawaii, it takes time to learn to separate disaster from pleasure.

That night, when Ivan's departure was still new, the electricity went out in my house and I walked down the road to my friend Alapai's house, which was where we always gathered during the storms. Alapai and I had been best friends since childhood, and we had the kind of ease that comes from knowing someone most of your life.

That night, Alapai told a story to those of us gathered at his house. He said that there was once a Hawaiian girl who was visited by a lover from the sea, a shark god. And he came to her at night, no one knew how. Perhaps he slipped into her dreams and got her pregnant that way.

Everyone laughed, and someone turned down the hurricane lamps.

Alapai smiled at us. "Everyone needs a beer for the rest of this story," he said, his eyes shining in the faint lamplight. Fake groans went around as we all reached into the ice chest and pulled out a beer.

He continued, asking how could the girl tell her family? She was a virgin, after all.

Alapai's niece asked what a virgin was, but no one answered her.

And still, the girl's womb swelled. Her father wouldn't speak to her, just looked at her with eyes gone red from crying, and her mother took her aside and tried to get the truth out of her by tearing out big handfuls of her long black hair.

Alapai's niece said she didn't believe the story.

Alapai shrugged, and said that sometimes the truth was so unbelievable that everyone turned their back on it, just as the girl's mother turned from her, because she heard something in her daughter's voice, some kind of uncertainty that sounded to her like guilt, but was actually fear and wonderment. Falling in love is like that, Alapai said.

Several people objected, said love wasn't like that at all, but I was silent. I agreed with Alapai.

The wind was stronger now, and the screens slapped against the windows, and Alapai's deep voice was the steadiest thing in the world.

When the girl gave birth to a shark she was the

only one who wasn't surprised. Alapai said that her parents begged her forgiveness and of course she forgave them, because that's what you do, right? Her mother forgot that she'd ever pulled her daughter's hair, and they let her eat at the table again, her baby next to her, splashing in a bucket full of seawater.

When the girl recovered from the birth, the first thing she did was weave a blanket of thin green limu, a seaweed wrapper for her baby. She tried to keep it with her, but the baby shark was restless from needing the sea. It was homesick for something it hadn't experienced yet, had only dreamed about, in fact.

Alapai looked at me.

The girl built her baby shark a small pond in back of her house and it lived there, swimming up and down all day and all night, but still it didn't get well. So she finally took her baby down to the water where she'd first caught the eye of the shark god with her strong body, her long black hair. She carried the baby out into the water and gradually eased it forward. It hesitated for a moment, sensing for the first time all that water in one place, and it turned back towards her, frightened. She had braided a necklace of her long black hair for the shark, and now she put it around its neck so it would remember her. She pushed it hard, away from her, as hard as her mother had grabbed her hair, this was her family's way. Then she let it swim away from her. Her heart broke, but what else could she do?

From then on the baby shark was her family's 'aumakua, and protected them from harm. And when the girl swam in the sea, sometimes the shark would swim just under her, like a shadow.

Alapai ended the story there. His niece crawled up in his lap, teasing him for a sip of beer. The hurricane lamps were turned back up and a game of poker started.

I knew how the story really ended. The man-shark learned all he needed to know and then he disappeared for good. I wasn't sure which was worse, to leave or to be left behind.

The need for pleasure is the first thing we deny when a love affair is over. I was in mourning for Ivan, but it was the end of the pleasure I missed so much, even if I kept it hidden under all the other losses.

Before long, everything around me had turned into the shape of Ivan's body. The man ferns deep in the forests, the hunched shoulders of wet rocks under waterfalls, even the iwa birds crying at night became the sound coming out of his throat.

He'd left behind too many scents as well. The lotion he rubbed into his hands each night to take out the dirt of the elevator grease, the maile lei that smelled like his skin. I used up his lotion and bought more of it.

Eventually, his leaving turned into a time of invention, when I was comforted by making up my own versions of what had happened. I saw Ivan as a great flower I carried in my head; this hybrid, this Ivan-flower that I'd made by crossing the time he'd been gone with what I chose to remember about him, what I chose to ignore.

My mother would have just bought a new gun and gone hunting. Married a new man. Found herself a new target.

4

I come from a line of women whose husbands have all disappeared. The lucky ones were driven off or ran away, and the unlucky ones died before they could do either.

My mother married often, as did her mother before her. It wasn't carelessness on their part so much as a kind of unwarranted optimism that you see in unlucky gamblers, cardplayers who continue to bet on one losing hand after another. Folly in one person could be called high hopes in another.

When I was small, before I'd learned to read, I

picked out new husbands for my mother from the post office's most-wanted list. Since they were the most-wanted I believed them to be the best of men, the most loved. I'd stand on the wooden bench and leaf through the photographs while my mother picked up the mail. Some of the men were dark, like my father, and those were my favorites, though I was partial to anyone whose face appeared again and again, week after week. The Japanese had once had mail-order brides, and I thought these wanted men were somehow the same.

As I learned to read and the most-wanted list took on new meaning, I still leafed through the photos every week. I couldn't put down the notion that these were still desired men, even if they spent their time racing around the Mainland shooting people and counterfeiting money. I thought that perhaps my father would do something equally bad, and show up on the list, and I would at least know where he was.

Still, it was important to read the fine print on a person, something my mother's husbands had all neglected to do. She was not one of those lovable eccentrics making guava jelly for the entire neighborhood, her hair bundled up into a scarf. Her eccentricities had a sharp edge to them, she didn't care who saw what she was, and for that I forgave her almost everything.

While no one who knew her would have called

her sweet, or anything remotely resembling motherly, I was still too young when she died, and in my life so far I'd already missed her more years than I'd had her.

Most facts change as you get older, become something else. Her death was my fault. Many children believe that the death of their parents is somehow their fault, but in my case it was true. During the tsunami, when Hilo was swallowed by waves, she threw down another losing hand, and I didn't save her when I had the chance.

5

*W*hen I was a child, I fell in love with a dead man, the explorer James Cook. I didn't think of him as a hero. It's the devil who captures your heart, and to me Cook was a bad-news messenger from the other side of the world. He was a man with the black wings of the eighteenth century, an uninvited guest who made the world suddenly larger and more horrible than people were prepared for. He opened the door and the future came tumbling through and there was no going back.

Cook was killed on the Big Island, on the other side of the island from where I was born, and since the dead belonged to everyone, so he belonged to me. No one else did. My father was just one in a long line of men who had disappeared from my mother's life, and my mother rarely lent herself to me, spending most of her free time hunting in the mountains. Where we lived up in Volcano we were isolated enough that I had few visitors, no play-mates other than Alapai, only occasional electricity.

In his rush to get away from my mother, one of my stepfathers left behind his entire library, which was where I found dozens of books on Captain James Cook. The way a lonely child devours every book in the house, I read each book on Cook, even the ship's diaries, and so became privy to the oddest kinds of knowledge.

What I admired most about Cook was that he had the long view, he could wait years for what he wanted. I told myself that I'd be like that, as well.

My mother, on the other hand, could barely wait ten minutes. For her, a bullet took too long to reach its target. When my mother and her current hus-band screamed at each other, with the sound of plates or lamps breaking, her two favorite volleys, I was far out at sea, dancing a soft jig across sea-weary wood with Captain Cook, a man who'd buried the farmer's son under white cotton, who hid his black wings under a starched naval jacket, just as the shark-man hid his jaw from view when he came on land.

6

*D*own at the harbor, the fishermen said that Nicholas had worked hard for a haole boy from the Mainland, that even if he seemed a little silly in his safari hat, he'd kept up with the work. Later they said a lot of things, but on the way back in, on his very first day, Nicholas decided to jump off the boat before they came around the breakwater.

The captain warned him not to do it, but he was over the side so quickly that there wasn't time to tell him why. After a day of sharks following the boat, the men didn't think he needed a warning. Nicholas yelled from the water that he'd swim in from there, his arm waving to the men on the boat, who were gesturing at him to come back, but he was from somewhere with lakes, not an ocean, and the boat was too far out.

Before they could turn the boat around to pick him up, the high fin of a shark was already coming from the opposite direction, heading for Nicholas faster than the boat with the engine at full throttle. He had his hand up, waving; he never saw what was behind him, and his arm twirled in the air as the shark attacked, and he yelled, just once.

The captain of the boat drove up the mountain from Hilo. I was working in the greenhouses when I heard his truck pull up. He came in and rearranged the rows of protea and pulled dead leaves off plants until I stared at him long enough for him to stop moving and tell me that Nicholas was dead.

"What do I feel?" I asked him. It was the first thing out of my mouth.

"Hey, I don't know, Kinau. *I* don't think I'm feeling anything at all," he said, "but look." He held his hand out and it quivered, and we both stared at it, stupidly, until he put it down again.

"Why would he jump overboard?" I asked.

He shook his head. "No one can figure it. Maybe he thought he was safe once he was near the harbor."

"It doesn't make sense."

"No," he said, "it doesn't."

There are people who linger around disaster, and there are those who can't get away fast enough. The captain was the latter. When I heard his truck downshifting for the final curve in the driveway I was still standing in the same place, a pair of small clippers in my hand. I listened to his truck building up speed on the highway and the birds calling back and forth, and then it was quiet.

I went into the house and sat down next to the phone. What I had to do next was call Ivan and tell him that his stepson was dead. I sat in front of the phone, not wanting to call him, waiting for it to ring instead, for Ivan to have miraculously been told by someone else. I hadn't talked to Ivan in years, except in my mind. Sometimes I put words in his mouth, mostly having him beg for forgiveness. Words of remorse. Love.

But the phone didn't ring, and when I called his home all I let him say was hello, and then I said, "Nicholas's dead, Ivan, and I'm so sorry." I didn't know how to warm people up to bad news. All I could do was squeeze my eyes shut and jump.

"Why?" Ivan said, after a moment.

Which why? I wondered. Why was I sorry, or why was Nicholas dead?

"Loss of blood," I said finally, thinking of Nicholas's arm waving. "He died from loss of blood."

"What the hell does that mean?" Ivan said, and then I told him all of it, all except the scream, and the waving.

I wanted to leave it at that, get off the phone. I hadn't heard him crying like that since he'd left five years ago with Nicholas's mother. I wanted him to hang up and do his crying with her.

On the Big Island there are places which are marked for death, where the land itself waits like a hungry mouth. The sharp curve of highway up on Polipoli Pass that caught hold of teenagers driving late at night, the constant threat of the volcano erupting, the riptide at the edge of the bay, the rows of poisonous oleander trees planted too near a barbecue pit in the public parks, where sometimes a visitor broke off a branch to roast a hot dog and was dead before the second bite.

I drove down to the coast not far from where Nicholas was killed, where my mother had drowned during the tsunami that washed through Hilo like a nightmare. In that place, I took off my zoris and walked along the shoreline and sat down on a rock with my feet in the water and I thought surely a landscape must be worn down by what happens in it. But the day was peaceful, the water beautiful, the boy dead.

It was a bay not unlike Kealakekua, where James Cook had been killed, the same sweet curve of land, the waves spending themselves on the rocks and pulling back down into the ocean. I couldn't see that we'd come very far from Cook's time, when whether you lived or died was a mere accident of geography or timing, a tsunami that killed one person, a lava flow that curved at the last minute, saving another. A boy who could have jumped off a boat anywhere else in the world but there.

It was Cook who first showed the mouth of a hungry place, who carried the known hell of the eighteenth century across the Pacific Ocean to this island, where a boy had died because he didn't know any better, where Cook had died two hundred years earlier because he was certain he did know better. Where my mother had died for reasons I still didn't understand.

7

*N*icholas's death was a blade that sharpened all our nightmares, reintroducing night sweats and unidentifiable noises. The peacocks that wandered up in the hills above my house had once sounded like birds, but now sounded like babies crying. Even the bushes that rubbed up against the screen became the fingers of a stranger, scratching to get in. Sometimes at night I'd wake up with the roar of the water still in my ears, all these years later the sound of the tsunami still deafening my dreams, and the same panic was on me instantly.

I was running up the street in Hilo, everyone was running to get away from the water. There was nowhere to run to, nothing to climb up on, it happened so fast.

There was just one warning bell. We waited for the next bell, the way it had always been. Someone said that there was a new system to the warning bells, but others disagreed. Finally no one was sure whether one bell meant that everyone should evacuate, or whether it meant that everything was fine. But then there wasn't another bell, just the wall of water rushing towards Hilo.

My mother was parked in the street under a banyan tree big as an old elephant with a thousand swaying trunks. She was trying to start the engine of her flooded Nash. She must have known it was hopeless. We were in the middle of Hilo, in the middle of the street, in the middle of the night. I was seventeen years old.

Everyone was running past us, heading uphill. I could hear the soppy wet breathing of children, not quite crying, being dragged uphill by parents who were.

I got out of the car.

"Come on," I yelled at my mother. Come on, come on, come on.

Far out at sea a huge wall of a wave was climbing right across the surface of the water, and the bay sucked back like an old man's gums.

My mother said she was not getting out of the car.

She jammed her fist down on the horn. It was a ridiculous gesture, just another noise. There was already more noise than an ear could hold.

I couldn't see her expression in the dark car, just her long white hair pulled back in a bun, fist jammed into the horn. I imagined her snarling over some worn piece of lauhala matting.

Someone ran past us, screaming that a big one was coming, couldn't we hear it?

I heard everything, even the blood in my ears was deafening me. I ran around to the driver's side of the car, yanked open the door, and pulled on her arm.

The water jumped up to my knees.

I got in the passenger side, shut the door behind me, and braced my back against it. I pushed against my mother with my feet, trying to shove her out of the car. She was staring straight ahead through the windshield, her fist still on the horn, like a child unable to stop making the wrong gesture, someone who wanted to greet disaster with the noise of a carnival.

Water filled the floor of the car. I lunged, grabbed her arm, but she ripped herself free and I was holding the printed sleeve of her muumuu. A piece of outrigger canoe. A palm tree beneath a quarter moon.

The water surged up around her waist, I couldn't understand how it was happening that fast. She took one hand off the steering wheel and slapped me hard on the face.

She slapped me again.

"I'll do it my own damn way," she yelled. "Get out of the car yourself."

I went for her throat as a wave rushed through the car and pushed us up the hill about half a block. A green arc of light jumped across the night sky, and everything around us turned a brilliant bright green. The walls of the buildings, water, the people around us were all outlined in green. I saw my hands around my mother's neck and let go, and then everything went dark, every streetlight, every building. Nothing made sense.

A horrible sucking noise, a long slurping sound, was everywhere, and I was pulled out of the car and dragged down the hill towards Hilo Bay.

I tried to grab a pole or a street sign, but I couldn't see through the water. I hit something hard, fell down through deeper water, and started swimming without knowing which way was up. Finally I kicked up to the surface into air so wet that the only way I knew my head was out of water was a lantern shining somewhere. I saw the light and opened my mouth to breathe.

Someone slammed into me and hung on, and I tried to twist myself free but I felt feet on my back, shoving me under the water, pushing me down like a piece of wood to climb up on. Under the surface, I rolled around, grabbed his leg, and pulled him down as far as I could. I used his body the same way he had mine, by pulling my knees up to my chest and shoving off of him.

I thought I was free of him but he came up for air right next to me, gasping and choking, and I slugged him as hard as I could.

He grabbed on to me again with hands that were larger than my head. We stayed like that, hanging on to each other, using up each other's air, both of us trying to get enough strength to push the other one down under water. Then he let go of me and I was pulled along with the current down into the Wailuku River, but at the same time it couldn't have been the river.

My legs tangled up in thorny bushes and I took a deep breath and went under and pulled the branches up out of the ground, and dragged the whole bush with me, tangled up in my leg and cutting into my skin.

I heard a voice, but everything was too noisy. Something bumped my leg and I thrashed away from it.

I felt someone grab my wrist, and twist it. My other hand found his neck and squeezed. I brought my mouth up to his hand and bit as hard as I could.

He dropped my hand and yelled. Then he said,

"Quit fighting me, I'm on a surfboard."

I reached towards the voice until I felt the edge of the board, and I grabbed on to it with both hands. I was too exhausted to heave myself up on it. I just rested my face on the edge, the bush like a lobster trap around my leg. There wasn't enough air, the air was too full of water, and the waves roared, but after a while the noise seemed farther and farther away. There was just the wind and the water moving us out to sea.

Finally I pulled myself up on the board and kicked the branches off me and put my head down on a leg. The other man is dead, I told myself, that's why he let go of me. This is a different man, I told myself.

My teeth chattered when I asked where we were, and the words came out in gurgles.

He didn't know. He thought we'd come out through the bay, but that seemed impossible. Everything seemed impossible.

I felt the inside of my mouth with my tongue. I had several loose teeth, and one dangling by a thread of skin.

I told him I had left my mother in the car, and I was hoping the waves had pushed her car uphill.

He said she was probably okay. He didn't sound like he believed it.

The coastline was entirely dark, the sky clouded over. We were in a black box, being pulled out to sea. The farther we were from Hilo the better it felt. We might be down as far as Laupahoehoe, I said, but he didn't answer.

Later, I woke up in the dark, disoriented, with the man's hand holding my head steady. My tooth was lying in the side of my mouth and I spat it into my hand and started crying.

He said it would be okay.

I reached down in the water where he was hanging on the edge of the board, and I pulled him up so that he was halfway on the board as well.

I was still crying, but it was coming out like laughter.

"Everything's going to be okay," I said, because it was my turn to say it.

For the first time in my life, I felt like I didn't have a chance in the water.

Gradually it got lighter, the walls of the black box turned gray, and the outline of the island slowly became visible. We were surrounded by debris. Plastic bottles, pieces of wood and trash, lawn furniture. Coconut fronds floated in the water, but there were no people.

The tide sucked us closer to Hilo. A helicopter passed overhead but the pilot didn't look down. I felt the hole where my tooth had been.

When there was more than one color in the water I turned and looked at his face for the first time.

He smiled, weakly. He'd been dragged right over

some kind of fence. There were deep long cuts in his skin, about an inch apart, and in places where they'd gone deeper the white of his muscle showed. He had long, thick black hair and his eyes were gold and bloodshot.

We drifted for about another hour. I thought about sharks. No one came to help us, no one was looking this far out. The man was now immobile and bleeding heavily, and I pulled him all the way up on the board and hung on the edge and put my palms over the worst of his cuts, like a bandage.

After a long time I heard a small outboard motor.

I yelled and waved. The dinghy turned and headed in our direction. He didn't hear them coming alongside, and barely knew that two men were pulling him on board the boat.

I climbed into the boat too, and one of them lifted up the surfboard. "Lucky," he said, nodding at the board.

There was a wash of blood across the surfboard, and it dripped into the bottom of the boat and turned pink in the pooled seawater. One of the men took off his shirt and wrapped it around the worst of his cuts.

"Who are you?" he asked. He looked worried.

Neither of us answered.

"Are you from Hilo?"

"Let it go," the other man said.

We came in north of Hilo, and they moored offshore and floated him in on the surfboard and then carried it like a stretcher from the beach. Everywhere the trees were knocked down, and cars were half buried in mud.

Some people ran out to take care of him and I was taken into a house that hadn't been touched. Even the stairs on the porch were dry.

I told them that I had to find my mother, but they said the streets were blocked and the phone lines were down.

The man who'd pulled us into the boat said that it would be like 1945, that the bodies of the drowned would be lined up on the sidewalk outside the mortuary.

The other man looked at me quickly and told him to be quiet, but then I asked about the green light that had flashed across the sky, they said it was the electrical plant blowing up, and then I was asleep.

8

*T*wo days after the tsunami I was in Hilo, making my way slowly past fish lying on bits of sidewalk, fish half buried in mud, fish impaled on the edges of aluminum siding. I walked slowly, favoring my leg that had stitches in it I didn't remember getting. Sometimes I only guessed where the streets had been, or which buildings had turned into the air I was walking through.

My mother's car had disappeared. I asked everyone if they'd seen her green Nash but they just shook their heads or hugged me, which meant something worse than no.

Parking meters were flattened against the road like a kid's sucker. Some houses had lifted and traveled several streets over, untouched, while others had disappeared completely, leaving broken plumbing sticking up from cement foundations.

Up the street two drunk men were pulling jammed cars apart. Someone passed around hot jasmine tea laced with whiskey and I had a paper cup of it.

I still saw her driving away. Just letting herself be carried away, that wasn't like her. She was a fighter, a woman with an attitude that had disappeared when I needed it most. I'll do it my own way, she'd said, and slapped me hard on the face. I'd gone for her neck. What if she had died because of that, because of me?

I retraced my path, past people busy pulling furniture out of the mud. A woman found an unbroken water glass and held it up, smiling at it as I walked past.

Around the corner was the mortuary. There were bodies out front, just as the man had said. A long line of muddy dead people with rinsed-off faces. My legs went out from under me, and I leaned against the side of a building for a couple of minutes.

I didn't recognize any of them. None of them had her long, beautiful white hair. They were all younger. A child on the far end had an expression of complete horror on her face. I didn't know whether it was fear or just being dead that had twisted her face like that. I knelt down, touched her skin. It was hard.

Two men brought out the body of a man and laid him down at the other end of the line of bodies. After they went back into the mortuary, I put both of my hands on the little girl's face, I didn't want her family coming down to identify her and seeing that expression.

Her face wouldn't move. I couldn't get her lips to close around her teeth, or her cheeks to come down out of the wide yell that had sent her skin back towards her ears. I hung on to the dead girl. She started crying, but then I realized it was my tears covering her face.

A woman lifted me up and walked down the street with me, away from the bodies. I tried to apologize, but I was having trouble talking through the hole where my tooth had been, I was gurgling, the way I'd spoken to the man on the surfboard.

Finally all the dead people were put into a deep freeze, and when there was time to bury them, it was discovered that the bodies had frozen together, as closely wedged as the cars that had slammed into each other all over Hilo. The bodies had to be chipped apart with an ice pick.

My mother would have liked everything about it, but that wasn't what happened to her. She washed back into Hilo Bay a week later, a week that lasted forever. She would have liked to wash all the way up the watery streets of Hilo, her dead arms paddling up the streets, but she only made it to the edge of the bay, her body hauled out by fishermen who were so weary of death that they kept on fishing, bringing her in only when they'd filled their quota, when the hull of their boat was jammed full of fish and my mother.

I hadn't shut the car door and it disappeared for good. The banyan tree was still there, where my mother had parked under it, the long roots falling like thick rope from the branches, and the time for me was blurred and slow and unhappy.

Several weeks after they found my mother, the man on the surfboard called, said he'd been trying to find out my name. He said he needed to see me, told me his name was Ivan.

9

---

*T*ime is like an accordion, that's what Cook believed, that's how he could stand spending so many years in a boat. Most people say that pleasure passes quickly but they haven't yet learned to play time's instrument.

Here is my love, arriving at last, my pleasure. I pull the accordion ribs wide, this moment will last and last. And here is a dark time whose events I place between my hands and squeeze together, forcing time to rush like wind.

10

*W*hen Ivan first courted me, it was through photos of disasters: I'd line them all up, the burning building, the local wedding that lasted longer than the marriage, the house slipping off the cliff into the sea, the children dancing in the busted water main.

He set up a time and place for us to meet, but I didn't go. I wasn't willing to be in some dreary survivors' club. I didn't need to see him to be reminded of what I'd lost in the tsunami.

I made my own way, kept my mother's plant

business going, found out why she should have been exhausted, didn't find out why she never was.

At the end of the day, I often sat in the greenhouses and watched the way dusk pulled the plants away and then later the way the night gave them back. The trees turned black and hunched down over the glass roof like large animals, and then when the color of the sky matched the darkness of the trees, they'd slip away into the night. Whoever thought dusk was a calm time of day hadn't ever seen this.

Then I'd turn on the misters, take off my clothes or not, and lie down on the cool cement floor as I'd done as a child watching my mother's long legs stepping over me.

So I missed my mother, but I got by. I kept my hands on what she'd left behind. A long braid of auburn hair I'd not known of, curled like a snake in a box on her closet shelf. I cleaned and oiled her guns. I discovered that she kept her money in the pockets of her old muumuus hanging in the closet.

I found a photo of her as a child, taken in Makawao, over on Maui, at a target-shooting competition. A smiling barefoot girl in a brand-new muumuu and a coconut hat, her hands cradling a rifle, eyes already on some target beyond the photographer. My tutu stood next to her daughter, looking as thin and worn as my mother might have been if she'd reached that age. Tutu was holding up a strip of paper, which, when I looked at it with a magnifying glass, turned out to be a first-place ribbon.

Even in the photo, my mother's finger was crawling towards the trigger.

Finally Ivan sent a photo of his own hand. Just a hand, floating in space. He must have photographed it right after the tsunami. There was a long scratch and then a curve of small indentations, like a crescent moon, in the area between his index finger and his thumb. I looked at it closely, realizing it was a print of my teeth, where I bit him before I knew he wasn't going to drown me. Somehow I confused that with safety.

It was the hand that made me open the door to him. Later, it seemed to me that his hand was a trick, a way of making me believe he'd be that open as well. But you can't ask for what you yourself can't give. I'd never met anyone who hid as much of himself as my own family did, until I met Ivan.

11

*A*fter several stepfathers, by the time I was a teenager, my own father had receded, become as vague as those blurry shots on the post office wall I'd been so hopeful about as a child, those men caught in the middle of a mistake, the middle of their lives, not old, not young. Whenever I asked about my father, my mother told me that she had no idea where he was, he'd just disappeared. Into thin air, she'd add, snapping her long fingers. Thin air. A country all its own.

I didn't have that trick of James Cook's, I couldn't

yet pull the past into the present to keep it alive.

When I was fourteen my mother came into my bedroom one morning as I was getting ready for school and told me my father had died in the Midwest, in the town he'd been born in.

"Topeka," she said.

Outside, the rain whipped sideways in the wind, straight into the window.

"Topeka," I repeated. I'd never heard of it. I wasn't sure how to act. I was used to his disappearance, but not his death. My mother awkwardly patted my shoulder, with the soft slaps she used to reward her hunting dogs. It was clear she didn't know how to act either.

I looked up Topeka in a geography book at school. It was odd to think that I could learn the population, the kinds of birds, the amount of rainfall that fell on that city every year, and still know nothing about my father, not even why he had died there.

I tried to picture him with one of the birds I'd read about, flashing a color outside his window as he was dying, singing a blue-colored song to help him into the next world. I told myself that Topeka was a wonderful city.

Several days later my mother came into my room with a large box held out in front of her, but I would not take it. I had no idea what was in it. For a moment, I imagined it was my father's body, neatly folded over and over until it fit into the box.

She held out the box, and I still didn't take it.

Finally she set it down on the bed, ran her hands through her hair, and looked like she was about to sit down alongside the box. I guess the look I gave her wasn't encouraging, and after pacing back and forth, she left.

I didn't want to open that box. From the way my mother was acting, I knew it mattered, and I knew that with my mother, when things mattered, they had a way of making you very unhappy.

When I did open it, I found years and years of letters and cards from my father to me. He'd left before I'd learned to read. There were birthday cards, postcards from trips he'd taken, even some menus from restaurants he'd enjoyed. We didn't have regular mail delivery up in the mountain, just the post office box, and my mother had always picked up the mail. I didn't know that he'd ever written to me.

It took me hours to read them all. On the menus he'd circled his favorite foods, put stars next to some dishes, and in big blocky handwriting he'd written things like "I sure enjoyed the meatballs," or "I'd never order the steak again, I asked for it rare and it came tough as a fifty-year-old cat." In all the letters, there wasn't a single recrimination from my father for never hearing from me. Perhaps he knew my mother much better than I did. It was a generosity of spirit I found nearly unbearable in a man I'd missed knowing altogether.

After I read each letter, I carefully put them back in the box, lining them up according to date, and then put the box under my bed.

I lifted one of my mother's guns off the rack and took a box of bullets, and went outside and walked downhill to the greenhouses, loaded the gun in the grass, then stood up and aimed at a pane of glass and pulled the trigger. The blast followed and the pane fell into the greenhouse with the sound of wind chimes. It felt good, so I shot another pane, then another. I walked around each greenhouse, reloading the gun countless times, seeing the panes of glass shatter again and again, not stopping until I'd used up the whole box of bullets. My mother had an endless supply of bullets, and there weren't enough things on earth for her to kill to use them all up.

When I finished, shattered glass covered all her nursery plants and the wind ran through the greenhouses, shaking each plant, and I wondered why, in all the time he'd been gone, my father had never thought to rescue me.

I went back into the house. My mother had disappeared when the shooting started, probably a wise move.

The box of letters was still under my bed, but I

didn't think it would be for long. I had a feeling
that my mother would get rid of them, so I took the
box with me and rode my bike down to Alapai's
house.

His mother came to the back door and opened it.

"Your mom's shooting, eh?" she said.

"Yeah. Target practice."

She raised her eyebrows. My mother was the last
person needing target practice.

I went down the hall to Alapai's room and
handed him the box, and he read each letter and
card carefully, in the right order, and he cried, but
I wouldn't.

My mother and I never discussed either the broken glass or my father's letters, which I kept hidden
away from home, under Alapai's bed.

She put up thick sheets of plastic until she could
afford enough glass to repair the greenhouses, and
even then we had to wait a long time for it to come
from the Mainland. After the new glass came, my
mother planted green ti all around the greenhouses
as a kind of insurance, because ti kept bad luck
away. She wasn't taking any chances, she muttered,
there could be another shipping strike on the Mainland and where would we be then?

As she swept the glass out of the greenhouses, she
gave me hints on which guns were better for closer

targets, which for long distances. I didn't forgive her and it took me a long while to figure out she'd never expected me to.

For years afterwards I wrote letters to my dead father. I sent them to the last address he'd used before his letters stopped. When you're writing to the dead, some facts seem more pertinent than others. Sometimes I enclosed drawings of flowers that were in bloom in the greenhouses, not the showy ones, but the delicate small flowers, ones he might have been likely to forget, the flowers my mother used to call the dirt underneath the steeple. The blooms you crush underfoot while reaching for the obvious prize.

In other letters I complained about my mother. The letters never came back, which comforted me.

James Cook's letters took years to reach his wife, and only then if he was lucky enough to run into a ship heading home. I tried to imagine writing a letter knowing it would take years before it was read, though I thought Cook had it a lot easier than me. Imagine writing to the dead, I would have told him, and yet for all the news he had of home, Cook might well have been.

Cook's wife burned all his letters shortly before she died, which I thought said a great deal about the passion that must have been in them. No one burned a letter in which one's health was asked about, the weather fine, hoping to hear from you soon. Letters of desire were the ones that turned black in the flame. The rest of it was window-shopping. No, his letters went something like this: I cannot bear being apart from you. I cannot bear it. I cannot.

12

*H*istorians love to write that after James Cook was killed, someone ate his heart by mistake, thinking it was that of a pig. Cook was the son of a farmer, he would have laughed at that story, because he knew a pig's heart was smaller, about the size of an angry fist. No, if they ate it, it was because Cook still had a little lick of immortality about him and the job of historians has always been to bring immortals down to the size of men.

But there was a little-known fact about Cook's heart. After years at sea, time itself curved his heart into the shape of what he longed for, and Cook's heart came to be shaped almost like the bow of a boat, a shape that could be perfectly cupped in the soft hands of his wife.

Perhaps people found it difficult to believe that such an adventurous man could be obsessed by his wife to the point where his heart changed shape because of her, and yet be able to leave her for years at a time, on long sea voyages. I understood this as a child, I understood it more as an adult. Cartography gave Cook the long view, that we are shaped more by absence than by presence. Distance itself is better understood as an equation of time and longing than latitude and water.

13

*A*fter Nicholas died outside Hilo Bay, Ivan called me constantly from the Mainland, and at first he made no sense at all. Then it was as if he had come up for air and his words were clear and sharp and hard.

Once he got me on the line, we played thirty questions. He gave the answers, I was supposed to guess the questions.

"I should have been there," he said.

I wondered how far back he'd like to set that

clock. Then he blamed Nicholas. After that he blamed me because I was the one who put him on the boat.

I didn't tell him that Nicholas had asked to work on a boat and I didn't tell him that I'd kept the fake driver's license for myself, the smiling boy with the added years slipped behind my own license in my wallet. Now that he was dead, it seemed important to memorize his face.

"You could say something, Kinau. You could say something to help."

But I couldn't. I didn't know what he wanted to hear, what would comfort him. I held the phone and stared out my bedroom window at the glass greenhouses that I'd shot out years ago and I thought that my mother had probably wanted to comfort me then, but there's no comfort to give for some kinds of pain. It has to go its own course.

"It didn't have to be like this," Ivan said one evening, and hung up. The next day, his tone had changed, his voice was clear on the line, and it made me nervous. I knew that tone well enough to be wary of it, his voice pulling like a strong tide.

"I've an idea," he said. "It's what needs to be done."

I waited.

"I'm putting a bounty on sharks. Cash, so much per foot. Hell, I still know a lot of people in Hilo and up the mountain as well. There's a lot of fishermen would show up for a bounty. A lot of sharks, a lot of money, it'll be good."

Before the end of the day he'd called around, and the word was out. Fishermen started coming into town from as far away as Kona and down the mountain from Kamuela, to make extra money. A few days later Ivan called to say that he was raising the price on pregnant sharks.

"Now, why didn't I think of that," I said, and from then on I quit answering the phone.

I set the sprinklers in the greenhouses on automatic, and stood in the soft mist until my hands looked like seaweed, my palms unreadable.

I drove the truck without having any destination, heading down the mountain to Hilo, where I drove slowly along the streets of the town that Ivan and I had both been raised in. I wanted reassurance that something was staying the same, but Hilo had shrunk down since Nicholas had died. A young boy dying made me feel suddenly old, as if my body had stiffened overnight.

I took a shortcut through an older residential area I loved, with miniature rock gardens in the front yards and small extended porches with rooflines curved as sweet as the Buddha's mouth. I drove past tackle shops and Chinese restaurants selling dim sum, which is the most beautiful food in the world, like a small gift held in the hand. The crazed pulse of birds came from the trees, and the canoe clubs were practicing in the water, the women in shower caps, their strong bodies leaning forward like dominoes.

Lili'uokalani Gardens was rebuilt after the tidal wave wiped out most of Hilo, and I drove under monkeypod trees that threw dark shadows of lace onto the sky, and I looked up and thought of reefs, of dense clumps of coralhead, of places that were safe and places that weren't.

The closer I came to the bay, the stranger Hilo became. The town was crazy with parking jams, photographers, fishermen hauling sharks through town, the long-dead sharks heading off in one direction, newly dead sharks heading the other way. It looked like the tuna cannery, with the white meat on one conveyor belt going one way for humans, the dark meat on another belt heading the other way for cat food. If you held still, the whole scene blurred. The trick to seeing it at all was to keep yourself moving.

I parked in the loading zone, the same spot I'd parked in as an underage kid driving my mother's old Nash—the only Nash on the Big Island—the same spot through my marriage to Ivan in a beat-up old Valiant, and now in an ailing Ford pickup that had to be left running or kickstarted. I sat in the cab with the engine idling, thinking how peculiar it was to consider my life in terms of cars. They always seemed to come out of it better than I did.

I watched the boats, and the point farther out where the water turned metal-colored, where the boy had died.

I wanted to think of Nicholas as a man now that he was dead. Why was that? I wanted him to be more than a boy, that was what it was, to somehow know that he'd had his time on earth. And I wanted to remember something particular about him. The way he carried himself, whether or not he was at ease in the world. The truth was, it was his tattoo that I saw most clearly, clearer even than his face, that ship rolling across his young flesh, the anchor without a name yet, the door to his heart still open.

It was a perfect tattoo for a boy his age, a sail full of wind, a way out of here. He would have become a lovely man, I thought, and then I didn't want to think of it anymore.

A cop walked back and forth in front of my truck, getting himself all wound up about my truck parked in the loading zone. He was new to the police force, and I could tell that he wasn't sure whether I mattered or not. I closed my eyes and tried to picture what Ivan's body looked like after these five years. I'd always loved Ivan's body, but it was how it felt that I remembered most. When I opened my eyes the young cop was still there. I thought of the stories of the shark-men. What if one of them had a twisted sense of tradition? What if he came on land as a young haole cop from the Mainland with only

a blue uniform to hide the jaw in his back? What if
the things those shark-men had to say were as ordinary as what Ivan had said to keep a woman in
an elevator from panicking? Would something that
ordinary save us? I wondered how the cop would
feel about lifting up his shirt, just in case, but then
we were both distracted by a boat coming into the
harbor much too fast, the wake spilling across the
water, sending the other boats bobbing up and
down.

They pulled up to the dock and tied off. I didn't
recognize either the boat or the men. One of them
held up three fingers. Three sharks. The other one
kept making triangular shapes with his arms. He
looked hysterical.

They'd found Nicholas's body, what was left of it.
The harbormaster came down out of his glass office
and helped the hysterical man off the boat and sat
him down on a wooden crate on the dock. Someone
else put a beer in his hand but he never even lifted
his head. Then they all had beers, the whole crowd
was drinking and people gathered and broke over
the three men, like waves.

I got out of the truck and followed the cop down
to the edge of the crowd. I saw it. I should not have
looked, but I had to, and what I saw was two men
holding what looked like gray wood gone soft in the
water, and I could not take my eyes off it, that was
the truth.

Even for people who had not looked, Nicholas would be remembered in ways that would give no comfort. The children in town would remember him as a haole boy from the Mainland who hadn't listened. The children themselves were sick of listening, and followed only those fishermen who weren't interested in lecturing them on safety, the ones who were busy making their own circles of blood.

14

*T*he following day I attached the boat trailer to the truck, pulled around in front of the greenhouses, and drove down towards the coast. The fields of sugarcane were bending in the early wind, waves of silver rippling through the cane like the skin of an animal, and the brick-red soil at the sides of the road was the dark fish color of a freshly gutted ahi.

At the harbor I parked in the loading zone and walked down across the parking lot to the harbormaster's office up on stilts. We had a cup of coffee and watched the trailers pulling up to the boat ramp in a minor early-morning traffic jam, and a man who kept throwing himself over an outboard motor, as though his body had turned into the piece of string he kept pulling out of the motor over and over again.

We didn't talk about the boy. Instead, both of us gave more words to the bad coffee than we ever had before. When there was an opening in the traffic jam I went out and backed my trailer down the boat ramp, slipped the rowboat off, and had a stranger hold on to the line for me while I parked the truck.

I rowed offshore to lay net. Although it was harder, I liked to lay net with no one else in the boat, just the rattling sound as I fed the weights over the side and into the water with one hand while I rowed with the other. The weights rattled like a rosary, and when all the net was out I tied plastic milk jugs at either end as markers.

The day was bright and quiet, the ocean as still as it was when I was a child rowing with Alapai on calm days, when we would time ourselves rowing between two points, and the sun would slide right over the flat surface of the water and into our eyes, the oars dipping down into the liquid mirror of childhood.

Alapai always let me row, which meant that it took forever and the boat filled with splashes of water as my small hands tried to navigate with the thick oars. Sometimes Alapai wouldn't talk to me, treated me like a haole, just another white person, or worse, a Mainland haole, the ultimate insult. Alapai's mother would stand on the beach in a long muumuu, her binoculars on us, taking swigs out of a bottle of ulcer medicine. She wouldn't swim, even though the 'aumakua for her family was the shark, and she'd be protected in the water. Why take chances, she'd say, adding that Alapai was using up all the luck in the family. I saw luck as something finite, something to be devoured and come to the end of.

Now I turned and rowed away from the island, straight out to sea. I rowed for hours, until the island shrank down into a squatting green frog, and my muscles grew and my arms seemed more attached to the oars than they did to my body, and then I turned around and rowed back towards Hilo without needing to see any of it.

I walked through the harbor after laying the net and passed by the King of Love on his usual street corner. He was shouting through his megaphone that there was a volcano erupting underwater, just south of the Big Island. As he spoke, he passed out plumerias and balloons. He had always called himself the King of Love, and dressed the part, in long capes and a cardboard crown from a fast-food restaurant. He said that this island had been growing and spilling lava across the ocean floor for thousands of years. Picture this, he said, it's going to take thousands more years for the volcano just to break the surface of the water.

His manner was urgent, as if the news he was giving us was timely. Without knowing it, I had probably taken my boat over that volcano, never feeling the reverberations of the hidden island building on the ocean floor.

His head disappeared behind the megaphone, reminding me of a bird dipping into a flower, as if that was where his sustinance came from, the yelling, the megaphone.

What if, the King of Love yelled, all this fire and change and land never becomes visible, never breaks the surface of the water? He looked at the crowd gathered around him and asked, what does one island know about the passion of its neighbors?

15

*A*s I pulled in the net, the fish beat against it, their scales still pure and bright, and I thought how the colors on land are just a poor imitation of the colors underwater. Even flowers can't compete against the colors of fish.

I'd caught more fish than I'd expected, mainly menpachi and weke, enough for Alapai as well. I rowed back into the harbor, loaded the net into the truck, and iced the fish down. Then I drove up the mountain to Alapai's house and made him coffee so

I could get him out of bed. I needed him to help me gut the fish.

We rode up to my house, carried the net full of fish across the wet grass into the backyard, and got out the cutting boards and knives.

The dogs were waiting, and as I sliced down the belly of each fish and reached into the cavity for the intestines, I threw them to the oldest dog, Kiko, who was a pup my mother had traded another dog for. For a wedding present, one of her husbands had given her a dog, a beautiful little golden retriever named Princess, which she immediately traded for a pit bull. Retrievers can't hunt pigs, she'd said, the notion of a pet simply not occurring to her. She'd let me name him Kiko.

Kiko scrambled for the intestines, his jaw snapping shut, guts and blood hanging off his chin, the sharp smell of blood in the air around us.

Alapai squatted in the grass and scraped off the fish scales, which flew everywhere, bright as drops from a hose, and stuck to our arms and faces. The dogs were in a half circle watching, but then they jumped up and ran towards the front yard as someone came walking around the side of the house.

I realized who it was in my legs first, then up into my chest and arms. Alapai glanced at my face, and I must have looked sick, because he came to me, put his hand on my shoulder, and took the knife out of my hands.

"What?" he said softly. "What's going on?"

I pointed with my chin and Alapai turned.

"Oh," he said flatly, "look who's here."

As Ivan walked up to us, he looked at Alapai and then back at me, then quickly back at Alapai as he suddenly recognized him. He nodded and Alapai nodded back. Alapai touched my shoulder again, to let me know he was with me, and to let Ivan know it as well, and then he threw the fish scaler down onto the grass, like a match ready to start a fire.

I looked down and wiped my bloody hands on the grass. I'd pictured many meetings between us, but not like this, when I was covered with blood and fish scales. And what I felt was what I'd always felt, as though I was looking in a mirror and finally seeing myself clearly. There was the same feeling between us, that slow, inevitable pull towards each other.

"Well," Ivan said, "I'm here."

Neither Alapai nor I said anything.

"I, um, rented a car and got a hotel room down in Hilo. Then I drove up." He looked at the fish. "I see you got a good catch."

"Yeah," Alapai said, "we got lucky." He motioned towards the net. I could almost feel his hands on me, trying to pull me back.

Ivan smiled. "Doesn't change much around here, does it?"

I heard Alapai take a breath and let it out slowly.

He'd never liked Ivan, said Ivan had the personality of a traveling salesman, someone whose mind was never in the same place as his body.

"Listen, I've got to get going," Alapai said. "See you later, Kinau."

"You want a ride?" Ivan asked.

"Nah," Alapai said. "It's not far."

"I know," Ivan said softly, too softly for Alapai to hear. "I know how far away it is."

He bent down and picked up the curved scaler Alapai had dropped in the grass and reached into the bucket for a fish. He scaled the fish awkwardly, as though he was washing clothes with a washboard, while I stood staring at the bloody smears my hands had left in the grass.

When he handed the fish to me I wasn't ready to see his face that close to mine, so I kept my eyes on his hand, on the curved scar shaped like a fishhook that ran across his thumb to the index finger. I picked up the knife and took the fish from him and sliced down the belly and slid the smooth yellow sac loose, dumped it into the bucket. We worked like that, without speaking or looking at each other, until all the fish were cleaned.

When we were done, I took the blunt edge of the knife and ran it down my arms to shave off the fish scales stuck to my skin. I handed the knife to him, and he held it in his hand a moment and then put it down.

Age had started pulling his color away, I'd seen

that in the first glance, white streaks in his hair that I had to look at twice to believe. I'd promised myself that his hair was still as black as the day he left me.

"Come on in the house," I said. It was the first thing I'd said to him and it didn't sound right, didn't sound the way I wanted it to.

"Sure," he said, and followed me across the grass.

I pushed open the back door, and he took a step in over the threshold, forgetting to take his shoes off, tracking in the dirt like a Mainland haole. He looked down at his shoes, smiled at me, and went back to the door to take them off.

He looked tired, and quite lost, and he stepped hesitantly, like a blind man coming into a room he'd lived in once. I led him into the kitchen, and he glanced around. Hibiscus painted on the walls. Green table and chairs. A mounted mahimahi that I had caught the year he'd left. Lauhala mats on the floor. He was still not talking, but neither was I.

I caught myself trying to fold my hands smaller and smaller.

"You're nervous," he said, and I stopped moving my hands.

"I want to tell you how sorry I am," I said.

He nodded. "Thank you." He held up his arms, still covered with fish scales. "Where should I wash up?"

I pointed down the hall, but he just stood there, so I led him into the bathroom as if he didn't know his way around. He stood with his arms at his sides, staring at his face in the mirror above the basin. Then he blew on the glass, fogging it.

"He saw this place, didn't he?"

"Yes, he spent the night here."

"Which room?"

"Down at the cottage."

"Did he see the greenhouses?"

"Yes."

"What did he like the best?"

The ocean, I wanted to say. He liked the ocean most of all, but I wouldn't tell Ivan that, it would just make things worse. "I don't know," I said. "He liked everything."

"That's how he was," he said, and blew on the glass again.

I imagined unbuttoning his shirt and pulling it off him, and taking his belt off. Then he would step out of his pants and he'd be paler, pale all over, which I somehow wouldn't have expected even though he lived on the Mainland, and the hair between his legs would be lightly flecked with gray, and I wouldn't expect that either.

Instead I handed him a towel, and he glanced over at me quickly and the look he gave me went into a kind of sweetness and back out again so fast that I almost didn't see it. I heard him turning on the water as I shut the door and left him in the bathroom.

So he's here, I told myself. What now? What are you going to do about it?

Under the outside shower I washed off the fish blood and breathed deeply, which was supposed to be calming, but it seemed to do the reverse. I dropped the soap, I swallowed water trying to breathe deeply, I was sick to my stomach.

I went out back and iced the fish down.

I remembered Ivan jumping off a high cliff with a ti leaf in his mouth to keep the water out of his nose. I remembered going mud-sliding with him, and the way his body looked, strong legs, beautiful shoulders, shooting down the trail like something whose strength would never leave. Now he just looked ill at ease in the world, and sadder than I'd ever seen him.

A moment later he was standing next to me with a towel around his hips. He stood as if deliberating, but it was a pretense, there was nothing to deliberate.

He took my hand and pushed it against the wall, and I resisted, and he pushed his thumb into my palm until he felt me give way. With my other hand I wiped a line of sweat that had formed above his lip.

We'd always known the parts of each other that belonged to us, the parts which were easy to offer: lips, cheek, wrist. But what of the soft inner part of the eyelid, or just under the eye, where when he was tired, Ivan's skin looked steeped in tea. What we didn't give to each other we left our mark on, as a remembrance.

I pulled him down the hall into the bedroom, and there was the Ivan I knew and didn't know, his mouth full of dangerous angles, the long blind curves and straightaways of his body, his hands that felt like they'd been warmed by fire, the thin ridge of the scar on his hand.

In bed his strong feet moved like boats. Everything in the world bent towards me at the moment when I took his face in my hands and looked at him clearly for the first time. Outside my window, the clouds, the 'ohi'a trees, the geckos in heat, their sharp lizard calls echoing from one side of the palm tree to another.

When I felt Ivan's body against mine, for a moment the dead boy hovered in the room, asking for our attention, but we wouldn't give it to him, not right then. We were too busy trying to find what we'd once had together, but that was gone and this was something new.

I held my thoughts still and felt my common sense fly out the window and perch under the eaves of the house, like a bat hanging onto a world gone upside down.

Ivan sat behind me on the bed, brushing my hair with long soft strokes through the heavy weight. I closed my eyes, thought of my mother brushing my hair when I was a child. Then he took the brush down my arm, lifted my hair, and lightly scratched the brush across the back of my neck. He pushed me down onto the bed and brushed my legs, my neck, my stomach.

He told me he had a hotel room down in Hilo and that he'd left most of his things there, and he asked if he could spend the night.

I made room for the dead boy, who was suddenly with us again, smiling in his safari hat, showing me his fake ID, his ticket into the adult world.

"Are you thinking of Nicholas?" I asked.

He gave me a quick glance and leaned forward and brushed my hair, then looked out from behind my head and into the mirror. "He was, you know, perfect," he mumbled.

The dead are always more perfect than the living, I thought. To me, Nicholas was still a boy looking forward to his life, and he was attacked by a shark. And his death ran through the town like something liquid. Something that left a high-tide mark on the walls.

"One of a kind," Ivan said. He stood up, carrying the brush, and paced back and forth, a motion that took only seconds in either direction.

"His mother will never get over this. She is . . ." He paused, searching for the right word. "Devastated."

I thought about this boy who was and wasn't his,

whose death left sharks under all the eaves in town.

Ivan sat down next to me on the bed. "You know what I want to do tomorrow?" he whispered in my ear. "Go hunting."

I got up and went down the hall and unlocked my mother's gun cabinet, and thought about which gun would be right for Ivan. None of them, actually. I pulled two guns out as Ivan followed me into the room.

"You know what I think about most? I remember Nicholas playing softball, he had those big feet . . . he was growing so fast, when I put my hands on his shoulders, I swear I could feel the bones growing."

I pulled out a box of bullets from the drawer beneath the cabinet and turned to listen.

"He'd go to bed and wake up an inch taller, he was one of those kids." He trailed off, awkwardly drumming the gun cabinet with his fingers.

I carried the guns out to the kitchen and set them down on the table. I wasn't sure when the gun I'd chosen for Ivan had last been fired, so I decided to clean it. I got it out and pulled a soft rag through the barrel.

16

I was up early the next morning. I made coffee and drank several cups while I put the guns into the truck and found my backpack. I called Kiko and the other dogs and fed them before putting them into the back of the truck.

The windows were black, it was still too early to eat, so I packed a little food in the backpack. I was hoping Ivan would change his mind about going hunting, but when I went back outside, he was already sitting in the truck.

I let the truck roll downhill in the darkness until

I'd built up speed, then popped the clutch and gave it a little gas as it started up.

"You should fix this truck," he said.

I downshifted for the last curve in the driveway, then once we were on the highway I steered with my knee and rolled the first cigarette I'd had in a long time. Alapai was trying to quit smoking, and he thought that if he rolled his own cigarettes, he'd smoke less. Now we were both proficient at rolling and he was still smoking the same amount.

We drove up the back roads into the mountain and the mud slapped up on the sides of the truck and gathered under the cab and let go with a slurping sound. The dogs jumped from side to side in the back of the truck, opened their mouths to snap at the cold morning air. Ivan kept one hand on me, moving from my breast to between my legs.

I didn't trust myself around him. My mind had gone on holiday. I glanced over at him, his sharp profile, dark hair striped with gray. What was it about how a person looked? A mouth that made no difference at all to the rest of the world, the curve of a nose, the amount of hair you could grab in one fist. Were these the things that decided your life?

On the trail, Ivan carried the gun across his back, with the barrel up. He switched to his right hand, then back to his left. He said it was hard for him to find a comfortable position for a gun that had belonged to my mother, and I laughed at that. She would have been pleased to think that all these years after her death she was still making a man uncomfortable.

We'd gone hunting only once before, not long after we'd married. He'd made so much noise that I'd thought it was on purpose, and when I'd told Alapai about it later, we both agreed that it was lucky for Ivan that my mother wasn't on that trip.

The mist crawled out across the ground and the air felt like something solid as I took it down into my lungs. Bony 'ohi'a lehua branches put a hand out through the mist, scratched our shoulders and arms, and disappeared. We were only about a quarter of the way up the mountain, and Ivan's breath was already labored. But at least the wind was blowing in the right direction, keeping our scent behind us.

When the dogs whined against their leashes, catching a scent, I crouched down and let them loose, and they flew out ahead of us, running through the ferns. A moment later they came flying back over their own tracks.

Ivan looked at me, questioning. I held a hand up: wait.

He looked ready to take about another ten steps, find a pig, shoot it, and be home for lunch. My mother said never hunt with distraught people, they confuse what they're doing with hunting.

The dogs veered off like trains switchbacking on the way up the mountain. I was more worried that the dogs would find a pig than not. Ivan didn't need the sight of dogs taking small nips out of a pig's hind legs, keeping the pig twirling like a top until one of us came in with a knife and cut its throat. I was hoping to exhaust the notion out of him.

I slowed down several times for Ivan to catch up. He came into view below me and pulled out a knife from his boot, a knife I didn't know he was carrying.

He was weak-kneed and out of breath, and he took the knife and stabbed the air in front of him with jerky movements, then swung around and stabbed the air behind him. He crouched, slipped the knife back into the sheath in his boot, and stood up, breathing hard. I didn't want this Ivan, a man half crazed for blood, trying to bury his sorrow in a knife blade.

My mother used to tell a story about a pig that could take on the shapes of other animals. This would have been a good disguise, except that the pig always took on the appearance of whatever the hunter really wanted to kill. A neighbor's cow, a goat, sometimes even people. Those were the hunters who went crazy, and shot at everything, and always missed the one thing they were desperate to kill.

It was still early, with the air cool enough for my breath to show. The cliffs looked like they were about to fall right over on us, and the dogs ran straight up into the shadows and disappeared. I could read those shadows on the mountain like a clock, I could tell him how many hours old his grief was, but there wasn't anything else I could do. Later in the day the cliffs would pull back into themselves as the light changed, and the green would slowly creep up the sides of the mountain, and none of that would help Ivan until he let what he was feeling change into something else.

Later, when he thought he was hidden by a cluster of tree ferns, he again pulled the knife out and swung it around in the air, over and over. As I watched, I realized that he was sticking it into a hundred charging pigs. The knife spun at the end of his hand, his hand spun at the end of his arm, the world spun around him as he turned and sliced the wind, which went off howling.

It was a pantomime of grief, a dance for a dead boy. But his grief wasn't bearable, it was an invasion, a takeover. And it wasn't going to balance the world for Ivan to kill a pig, it wasn't going to right the order of things. It was just another death.

I picked up speed, so that he'd have to labor to catch up, and the ferns scratched my arms and face, the mud tried to grab hold of my feet and pull me down under the surface. I was ready to do anything to make him human again.

I was sitting down when Ivan finally caught up to me. Neither of us said a word. At one time we'd flung our words at each other, carelessly. Now we had to think about what we weren't saying.

I took the knife out of his hands and put my arms around him. We were kneeling in the muddy grass and then we were lying down and my face was in the shadow of his neck where it was quiet. After a moment I moved down his chest and listened to his heartbeat, and he ran his hands through my hair.

Then I heard it, before Ivan did. I jumped up and ran towards the grunting of the pig.

The dogs tore through the brush ahead of us, cresting a hill and pouring down the other side. The soil was wet and each step was a slide. There was the humid sound of dogs panting, and my own breathing as I tried to keep up, and then again I heard a pig grunting way up ahead.

The low ferns scratched against my jeans, leaving a sharp grassy smell. I ran through the hapu'u tree ferns that threw a jagged umbrella of shade, and back down into the low fern and 'ohi'a. Two ridges over, the 'ohi'a were tall and beautiful, but on this part of the mountain they were scrubby bushes.

I didn't say anything when Ivan caught up to me, out of breath, the front of his jeans smeared in mud, where he'd fallen more than once.

I pointed to a low wall of fern, where pigs had rooted. The ferns were hollowed out into a bright green tunnel. Everywhere were the signs of the pigs ruining the forest, tearing everything up, exposing the roots of trees that would soon die.

I went on ahead, looking for the direction of the tunnel, but Ivan stayed behind, staring at the path. He dropped down on his hands and knees and pushed his way through the fern.

He held the knife in his teeth as he crawled, and I imagined the sharp taste of metal on his tongue. He transferred the knife to his hand, and it shook like a thin strip of aluminum roofing flapping in a storm. There was nothing wrong with that, it was good to be scared, but better to be scared with a steady hand.

The tunnel was probably an old lava tube, and I knew the pig would turn eventually, and come straight at Ivan. I pulled out the gun.

When the pig snorted, Ivan stopped crawling. The bushes moved as if they held a storm, and there was a whooshing kind of sound, and suddenly the pig came flying down the tunnel.

It was bigger than Ivan was on his hands and knees, and he held the knife straight out in front of him, but his hand zigzagged out of control and then the pig ran right around him as the knife slashed the skin on its side.

It squealed as it ran out of the tunnel. I shot it once in the head and then everything was silent.

Ivan came out of the tunnel backwards, slowly,

and when he stood up he looked at the knife in his hand and then down at the pig lying at my feet. I rolled the carcass over, showing where the knife had carved deep into the skin.

I dumped the backpack and found my tobacco and rolled a cigarette and handed it to him after I lit it.

I rolled one for myself and squatted down and turned the pig over to the unmarked side. It was a fully grown pig, a boar with slightly yellowed tusks and bristly hair.

The dogs whined to come close to the pig but I kept them away.

Ivan stared at the pig, smoked his cigarette, and didn't say anything. He pulled the tick-infested carcass up onto his back and started down the mountain with it. Like a cloak, I told myself. Like a warrior, I told myself. But I knew that was bullshit. The blood seeped through his clothes and the sharp rusty smell of it was in the air.

With Ivan carrying the pig, the trip down the mountain took a long time. He staggered under the weight, nearly falling several times, and once slid down a muddy hill with the pig nearly on top of him. He complained that the whole hunt had taken far too long and now he was stuck with this pig on his back.

It made me think about Captain Cook, who once,

while watching a dance of the creation of the universe, complained that it went on too long.

When we came to the dirt road where the truck was parked, I helped Ivan lift the pig into the bed of the truck, and I made him ride back there with it to keep the dogs away. When I looked in the rearview mirror he was smiling through a mud-caked mask.

On the way home I could have avoided the harbor, but there was something about Ivan's smile that made me turn at the last minute, take the road down past the harbor. There still weren't any parking spaces. Pickups were backed in sideways and the sharks that had been dead for a day were being hauled off in the beds of some trucks while newly dead sharks were being carefully unloaded off the beds of other trucks. Not even the fishermen could say why the newly dead sharks should be treated more carefully. It was just past training, the kind none of us could get away from.

Ivan stared at the sharks dangling from hooks, the bloody sidewalks. There was a congratulatory feel to the place. Everyone was a hero. We drove slowly past groups of fishermen who had no idea that the mud-caked man riding in the back of the truck was the one paying them for the dead sharks. When I thought he'd seen enough, when he was no longer smiling, I turned onto the road heading up to Volcano.

•   •   •

I poured the first pot of boiling water over the coarse hairy skin of the pig and began scraping hair off with 'opihi shells. The pig was pink-skinned under the hair, with black splotches like spilled ink, like a cartoon running across its skin. I remembered reading about a museum in Japan full of tattooed human skin, donated by people after they died. What tattoo would I choose for myself? A shark jaw, buried in my back?

Ivan was frowning over the pig, angry that he hadn't killed it himself. By now, he probably had the story twisted around where he would have done it if I hadn't stepped in first with the gun. Later, he'd be the one who'd pulled the trigger.

I kept scraping, pouring the hot water over the hide, ignoring the gash in the side, ignoring Ivan.

We hung the pig to bleed under the breadfruit tree, and I told Ivan that I'd had to shoot the pig, that there wasn't any other choice.

17

*T*he most violent act James Cook could think of was to take a ship through water. It sounded like nothing, a door opening and then closing. Yet even water has a memory, as does skin. The bow of a boat cutting through a wave, a hand running across a thigh.

History can say what it wants to about Cook, but the sneer must come off our lips, because history will say the same about the rest of us after we're gone.

A hundred years after Cook's death the missionaries pounded their wooden podiums in downtown Honolulu, their arms flying out, black sleeves hanging like the wings of mynah birds, their words preening and strutting, declaring Cook's corruption as the bored and hot congregation attempted to fan itself straight out of Sunday and into Monday. All this venom was directed at Cook because he allowed the Hawaiians to think he was a god. To think he was Lono, the god who would come at the time of the Makahiki.

First off, Cook didn't have much of a chance. Try denying you're a god sometime, when people are insisting otherwise. See how far that gets you. Skepticism sets in, people step back, touch the sharp edge of their weapons, wonder what good you are to them anyway. There's something infinitely clear about deciding how useful a person is. Cook had done it all his life, so he recognized it when he saw his usefulness dry up in their eyes. If you're paying attention, you can see the plans that death has for you.

Cook saw that he was singled out, that death was already taking a few quick jabs at his chest.

Most people aren't allowed to pick the exact moment of their death, the place. Cook had hoped for something quite different from the bay at Kealakekua, nothing so imaginative as that. Planning our own death, our original ideas are the first to fly out the window. We all want to die at home, in our own beds, with our loved ones nearby. Isn't that right?

And who hasn't secretly wanted to play God?
Isn't that the greatest seduction of all? Look at Saint
Theresa; there was a woman who knew what she
wanted. Nothing less than ecstasy.

So he played God a bit. Confess, you can't blame
him. Perhaps for Cook, that was what the marriage
bed was all about. Not the blushing bride, the hesi-
tant groom, but later, when what you're left with is
the physical hunger for your wife, when you try to
convince her that you're the only one right for her.
Only you can make her feel this, along the back of
her leg, the arch of her foot. Only your mouth
pressed onto her shoulder like this, your hand buried in her hair. Isn't that playing God?

Haven't we all at least attempted it? Cook's wis-
dom was mortal, therefore perishable, but at least
he knew this. Anyone would play God, given the
opportunity.

18

*T*here were no trade winds, just the dense heat, the kind just before a rain, the heat that slows down all movement, and even the geckos in the greenhouse were still, breathing shallowly, too hot even to hunt for flies, everything waiting for the rain.

I was transplanting mondo grass when Mr. Yamashiro tapped on the glass and came into the greenhouse, wiping his feet on the way in, something most people never thought to do. He complained about the heat for a while, and we agreed that it was hotter than any previous year, then he told me he'd driven up from Hilo with the cremation forms. He said he'd gone to Ivan's hotel with them but the desk clerk hadn't seen Ivan in a day or so and suggested he try my house.

I said it was a long way to come, all the way from Hilo.

He agreed, but said he couldn't just leave the forms at the desk of Ivan's hotel. "Too impersonal," he said, pulling out a handkerchief and mopping his face.

I wiped the dirt off my hands and accepted the large envelope of papers. "Ivan's up at the house, if you need to talk to him."

He shook his head. "I'm glad to give this to you, Kinau," he said. "I think it's easier for Ivan this way."

I agreed that it was and told him to pick out a plant for Mrs. Yamashiro, and he politely refused, so I took an orchid, wrapped the pot in newspaper, followed him out to the car with it, and put it on the floor of the backseat.

"Thank you, Kinau," he said. "You know she likes orchids."

After he left, I went back to the house.

Ivan was in the kitchen, examining the mahi-mahi mounted on the wall.

"Who caught this one?" he asked.

I set the papers down on the table, my hands leaving a wet print on them. "I did, when I was a kid. I've told you that."

Ivan smiled. "So, your mother ... and the taxidermist?"

"What?" I started laughing.

He nodded at the fish. "This proves it, beyond a doubt. They must have had an affair." He smiled up at the fish. "Why else would a woman like your mother go through an expense like this for a little kid?"

I was still laughing. "Because it was my first fish. My mother was big on firsts."

He raised his brows. "Your first fish? Hmm. How old were you?"

"I don't know, about eight?"

He gave me a look, and I realized I was being baited, that he was trying to ignore the cremation papers. He must have seen Mr. Yamashiro's car, which had his business name on both doors.

"Do you remember the taxidermist?"

"Sure," I said. "And you're right, he was a friend of my mother's, at least until she started taking every damn thing she killed down to him to be mounted."

"She wore him out," Ivan suggested as he took my face in his hands.

I'd forgotten how wonderful that felt, to be inside

Ivan's attention, and even if it was simply because he didn't want to deal with the cremation papers, I told myself otherwise.

I drew a line across his skin, and a small stream of sweat followed the path of my finger. It was the kind of heat that made me think of spontaneous combustion, of the surfaces of rivers that catch on fire.

The rains started suddenly, and Ivan opened the kitchen door and stepped outside. "Come," he called behind him, stripping his clothes off as he ran out into the rain. I followed and the thunder crashed and Ivan came around from the side of the house holding a bulb of shampoo ginger and he smashed it between two rocks under the eaves of the house until he had a handful of the thick plant juice, which he rubbed into my hair, and I closed my eyes and listened to the rain hitting the leaves like fingers snapping, the roar of it on the greenhouse roofs, the muffled sound of rain in the grass, while Ivan's hands washed my long hair, and then I ran shivering to the rain gutter at the edge of the house and rinsed the ginger out of my hair, and just as quickly as it had begun, the rain stopped and Ivan stood laughing in the middle of the lawn.

And then we were in bed and Ivan was still funny and I decided being in bed with Ivan was like being in water. Not weightless but somehow more buoyant, lifted, able for a moment to ignore the tug of gravity.

When I woke up, it was late afternoon and Ivan was carrying two mugs of coffee into the room. "Isn't this one of your mother's?" he asked, handing me a mug with a design of hunting dogs.

"Of course," I said, laughing.

He got back into bed with me. "Tell me about her," he said.

"You know all the stories about my mother," I told him, "including some I didn't know, such as this affair with the taxidermist."

He smiled and leaned back. Ivan loved to hear stories about my mother, but he never talked about his own family. He was embarrassed by the real estate deals his grandfather had made, taking a lot of money off people and feeling good about it, and his father was worse, having tried to build a luxury hotel on a sacred heiau, a burial spot. I remembered seeing his photo in the paper, getting himself photographed wearing an inside-out aloha shirt and a concerned look on his face, trying to appear benevolent while attempting to transplant the dead. But the dead don't move just because you pick their bones up, the spot doesn't become less sacred, even if the birds disappear for good.

We drank coffee and listened to the rain, and then I remembered a story of my mother's that I hadn't told Ivan, about her own grandfather. He'd sailed from the East Coast down around the tip of South America and up to Hawaii. He wasn't one of the topside missionaries riding for free. As my mother put it, he clung to the bottom of the boat like a water rat. Worked his way over, while the missionaries were all up on deck, drawing straws to see who'd take the best land in the islands. They said they'd keep what was theirs, my mother had told me, and their descendants were still saying it. God's will was a terrifically malleable thing in terms of Hawaiian real estate.

After that trip my great-grandfather hated even seeing boats. He said he'd used up a whole lifetime on that boat, and he'd refused to ever step into another. That was how we were all raised in the islands. He never even made it off Oahu. He told my mother that the things a boat brought were syphilis, mosquitoes, measles, and the Church.

I would have been a disappointment to him, because I loved boats. I'd watched them coming and going my whole life. Luxury liners looking like floating birthday cakes with all the candles lit, and the working boats trolling back and forth with a crown of gulls flying overhead. Long sleek canoes full of the best athletes in the world, men and women bending forward from the waist as their paddles pulled through the water. Then there were days when I'd see it with my great-grandfather's eyes and everything on the water just looked like trash coming in on the tide.

It struck me that my great-grandfather's boat had probably looked a lot like the tattoo on Nicholas's arm. But the boat on Nicholas's arm was full of sailors, cartoon adventures, and I knew that somewhere hidden in the hold there was a stowaway, a boy just his age.

"Hey listen," Ivan said suddenly, "we should go fishing."

"Fishing?"

"Yeah, let's go tomorrow. It's been years since I've been out on the water."

I hesitated, not sure that it was a good idea. But then I thought, why not? It made as much sense as anything else. I told him I could probably get Alapai's boat and decided to ask him about the cremation forms later.

The next morning, I slipped out of bed before Ivan was awake and went into the kitchen. The cremation forms were exactly where I'd left them. I looked for Ivan's signature, knowing I wouldn't find it. Until Ivan signed the papers, Nicholas's body was being stored in a deep freeze. Nothing further could happen to him, Ivan probably thought. Better this misery than the one that follows when the business end of death is over and he is simply dead.

I went out to the greenhouses and worked for

about an hour before receiving a call from Mr. Yamashiro down at the crematorium.

"I first tried you at the house, Kinau. It makes a good impression, two phone lines."

"Somebody better get impressed quick, I've got a lot of plants to sell."

"I know what you mean," he said, and I thought how I was waiting for things to bloom and he was waiting for them to die. Business wasn't good, all around.

When I told him Ivan hadn't yet signed the papers, he sighed.

"Ah, no?"

"I'm afraid not," I said.

"We must get him to sign. Today."

"Yeah, but that's easier said than done."

"He's gone?"

"Not exactly," I said, thinking of Ivan curled up in bed, the overhead fan clicking softly as it had done for years.

"Well, get him to sign, okay?"

"Sure," I said, as if I could do that.

19

We parked on the hill above the harbor and watched the fishermen who'd come for the bounty. I wondered if they found it possible to move closer to the boy when they killed a shark. I wanted to tell Ivan that I understood vengeance as well as anyone, but once it started it was never enough.

Alapai was down at the dock, talking to some of the fishermen. Ivan and I walked past the icehouse and over to the pier. While I was talking to the harbormaster, Ivan was asking Alapai for the use of his boat. I could see Ivan gesturing, saying something that mattered enough for Alapai to take a step backwards, fold his arms across his chest.

I made my way down to the dock. Alapai looked relieved to see me. Ivan just looked harassed.

Alapai shrugged, spread his hands. "It's a big boat," he said. "It takes two people to run it. Why do you want to take the boat out?"

Ivan didn't answer.

"He wants to go fishing," I said. "Catch a shark."

Alapai's boat had the sampan hull favored on the Big Island. It was a shape I'd known all my life, a shape I was at ease in. I jumped on board and checked the gas and started the engine while Alapai and Ivan got out the fishing poles and tackle. Alapai made a few announcements about the engine for Ivan's sake, and before I really had time to think about whether I wanted to be doing this or not, we were heading out of the harbor.

When we were farther out, Ivan took the gallon of slaughterhouse blood that Alapai had given him and poured it over the side of the boat to attract sharks. I knew I was basically an eye-for-an-eye kind of person, but that was before I saw the blood spreading in the water like a reef, like the canopy of a monkeypod tree. After a while it seemed that I was no longer smelling the blood, that instead it was smelling me. It was on me like the scent of a wet dog.

The smell of the blood mixed in with the smell

of the diesel engine. I felt queasy, but it was the wrong boat ride to be throwing up on. Backbone, I told myself. Stamina. I'd never thrown up on a boat in my entire life; I'd practically grown up on boats. I took the boat farther out, where most of the other boats were. It looked like a fishing tournament in full swing, with everyone festive and making money off Ivan.

I glanced at him, wondering if he saw it that way as well, but he was wearing a pair of Alapai's wrap-around sunglasses and a baseball hat and I could barely see his face.

The waves turned into swells and the color of the sea went from metal to turquoise, and when we were farther out, to navy blue. I felt like a complete fool, not even knowing if I was on the boat for the boy or for Ivan or for myself. I looked back at the island, the shape tattooed across my memory.

Ivan's line started whining, running out fast, and by the time he scrambled into the chair the fish had taken out over two hundred yards of line. I could tell he was nervous and almost gave up his seat, but then he stayed where he was, and I pretended that I hadn't seen him waver.

He braced his feet against the side of the boat and worked the shark. I knew it was a shark, because I didn't think it was possible for Ivan to go through that kind of effort for just a fish, not on this day, not even an ahi. We headed farther away from the other boats, and the sun was bright on the water, hot across my shoulders and arms. After about twenty minutes I went over and massaged Ivan's shoulders, and he said he felt like a damn tourist in a marlin tournament, and that made me laugh. Once I started laughing everything was funny, there was no stopping, but Ivan ignored me, let me wind up and play out like the fishing line.

I got his baseball hat wet in the water and stuck it back on his head. I figured he had to be getting tired, especially in his lower back.

He was still working the line, slowly gaining a little. I gradually changed direction, turning the boat around and heading back towards the island. The swells disappeared into waves and the water turned the color of metal again.

It was a long journey for what turned out to be just one small shark. I went for the captain's gaff and held the line while Ivan leaned over the side of the boat, and the gun went off. He grunted as he gaffed the shark and lifted it up over the side of the boat. He picked up the tail and gave the shark a shove and it slid across the deck. I felt like jumping overboard watching it head towards me.

After congratulating Ivan, I let him have the wheel. I watched the shark for a few minutes, wondering what I'd expected to feel about it and why I didn't. Then suddenly the shark flipped itself over next to where I was standing. I jumped up onto the hold and on my hands and knees I scrambled up again and turned to look at it. Once again the shark was still, its eye motionless. I found Alapai's baseball bat tucked behind the tackle box. I pulled it out and went over to the shark and clubbed it on the head, again and again, until I was sure it was dead and I could breathe again. And then I clubbed it some more, I couldn't stop, and the eye spilled out the way the stomach lining fell like fabric from the sharks that were hung up on hooks in town.

It was as scary-looking dead as it had been alive, with its fake-looking skin and face wound up tight the way I'd seen on people when they were getting ready to do something entirely crazy.

Ivan was watching me, and when I looked up his eyes went off to the horizon. He didn't say anything about the battered shark or my bloody knees and panicked breathing.

He looked out over the water and predicted our welcome back at the dock, and I wondered if the whole point of a bounty was to show you that you didn't know anything about yourself or anyone else. If so, I'd learned it.

We came into the harbor as it was getting dark, and the lights were turned on along the dock. The

dock was hosed down and pools of light shone on
the wet wood. It was a relief that most of the fishermen had gone home, and the few who were left
were busy preparing for the next day.

The harbormaster came down and shook Ivan's
hand, which embarrassed him. Ivan said the shark
wasn't part of the bounty, and the harbormaster said
he knew that, but it was still Ivan's first shark,
wasn't it?

They lifted the shark out of the boat and carried
it over to the scales and hung it up. Ivan wanted to
gut the shark himself, but I didn't want to see it, or
even find out how much the shark weighed. I told
him I'd meet him at home, and after cleaning out
the boat, I walked back up the hill and got into my
truck and went home.

Later that night, I woke up and realized that Ivan
wasn't in bed with me, that he must have gone back
to his hotel. I'd been dreaming about the shark, and
that took me back to a time when Alapai and I were
children. We'd gone around town and made all the
men lift up their shirts so that we could see whether
they had a shark jaw buried in the middle of their
backs. While some men had laughed, and pulled
their shirts up voluntarily, probably pleased to be
thought of in that way, others refused, and we'd tail
them through Hilo, trying to find out where they
lived. Sometimes we had to wait for them to go

swimming, or catch them doing yardwork on a hot day, and we were always disappointed to see their smooth backs. Relieved, but disappointed.

I wondered if Ivan had caught the wrong shark and whether it mattered.

20

*I*t was raining in Hilo, and the gutters filled quickly and the water began to fan out into the middle of the road. A woman ran past, coming out of nowhere and going back into it. I caught a glimpse of black hair plastered to her back, then took off my slippers and ran into the street. My lungs filled with the wet air, and I followed the clicking sound of her getas hitting the sidewalk as she ran somewhere up ahead of me, a sound like that of dice thrown down, or the click of a gecko.

I cut across to Hoku Street, where Ivan had called me from a bar. When I got there, Ivan was in the center of a group of men, exaggerating the size of the shark he'd caught. Nearly everyone in the bar was as damp as I was, shirts sticking to their skin, their hair wet. There was a smell in the room of clothes drying and another more pungent smell of warming flesh. Ivan looked like he'd been celebrating since he'd caught the shark the day before. He had dark shadows around his eyes and the skin there looked tender, worn. He looked at me without seeing me as I made my way through the men and slipped onto the barstool next to his.

"So here you are," I said.

"Here I am," he agreed happily, and signaled the bartender for two of what he was drinking. "Where else would I be?" he asked, smiling. "Everyone here is drenched," he said, looking into the mirror behind the bar. "Isn't that something?"

I told him Mr. Yamashiro was looking for him.

"You know, it'll surprise you, Kinau, but I don't remember every single person in this town."

Ivan was charming, I realized, without being particularly friendly. Up close, his charm could have a mean kick and a whiskey breath.

The bartender poured two shots of whiskey. I asked for a beer, and when the bartender brought it, Ivan reached over for my shot of whiskey and drank it down. In the corner of the room, the men gambled with dice thrown against the wall. Outside, the rain continued.

"Mr. Yamashiro runs the crematorium," I said slowly, as if he really didn't know.

"Ah." He swallowed his own shot quickly.

The longer I sat in that bar, the more convinced I became that if I'd said no to Nicholas, said that it wasn't a good idea to get a job on a boat, and what did he know about fishing anyway, the boy would still be alive.

I handed Ivan the consent forms for Nicholas's cremation and put a pen down on the bar next to his glass. He signed at the bottom of the page without looking at it, and asked if I'd hang on to the papers for him.

I rolled the papers up and put them into my coat pocket. I was hoping that once Nicholas was laid to rest, Ivan's life could take a course of its own and we could start again. It was the grief that was distorting everything, I told myself, needing to believe it.

Ivan lit a cigarette with a fancy matchbook from a restaurant on the Mainland, in a town whose name I didn't recognize. He set the matches down on the table and put the cigarettes back in his pocket. A simple gesture, but a way of reminding me that he had another life.

I was made miserable by a pack of matches.

The bartender set down another shot and a glass of beer, and when Ivan threw back the shot of whiskey I slipped the matches into my pocket.

Even in the bar, there was no getting away from what was going on outside. The mirror behind the bar reflected the window, and we watched the street as the sun came out and several men weighed two sharks for the benefit of the crowd before gutting them. A small group had gathered to watch the hanging, the weighing, the quick gutting that seemed to be getting even faster, the knife moving like a long zipper pulling open the shark's belly, the insides falling out like wet laundry.

The spray of blood freckled up the man's legs and the people pulled back as the circle of blood grew larger and splashed the sidewalk. I reached into my pocket, felt the hard edges of the matchbook in my palm, squeezed until it hurt.

I reminded Ivan that the cremation was the following day, and he nodded and asked if I'd go with him. I agreed, buttoned my jacket so the cremation papers wouldn't get wet, and left the bar.

The next morning I set two places for breakfast, two papaya halves and toast, two glasses of juice, as if that would make Ivan suddenly appear. I thought perhaps we'd misunderstood each other, but when I called the hotel, he wasn't there either.

With my dog Kiko for company, I drove down

the mountain through a light rain, the covering kind of rain that was like running after the mosquito truck when I was a kid, trying to stay inside that cloud of insecticide. If you couldn't see anything around you, the game was working. If you stepped outside the cloud of poison, you lost.

All the way down to Hilo I rolled cigarettes and smoked them without noticing, the cremation forms on the seat next to me, Kiko hanging his head out the truck window, his muzzle wet in the light rain. I counted signs, noted the color of mailboxes, mainly white, and saw that almost every anthurium was planted in a coffee can.

I parked on the incline out in front of the crematorium, hoping that there was enough slope to kick-start the truck after everything was over. Mr. Yamashiro was already waiting for me, his face bobbing up and down behind the fogged glass doors.

Peculiar courtesies are accorded to the relatives of the dead. Under the circumstances, I was as close to a relative as could be found, and before my engine was off, Mr. Yamashiro came running out in the rain with an umbrella. He opened it over me, took my arm, and led me gently up the steps, as if at any second I might disappear.

Inside the building, api plants rubbed against the glass of the windows. The leaves were large and covered the view and the daylight, like a green curtain.

Mr. Yamashiro told me how much his wife liked the orchid and asked me to follow him down the white-tiled hallway.

We passed several embalming rooms and I thought about the tree fern forests all over the Big Island that had been nearly wiped out because the Europeans had wanted the fuzzy inner parts of the tree ferns for their embalming. Then I thought of Ivan's mouth on the skin on the inside of my arm, the back of my neck, his fingers running down the small of my back.

In the back of the crematorium Mr. Yamashiro unlocked a door, and we went into an office and sat down on chairs that Mr. Yamashiro had painted the same pale green as the tiled hallway. I'd known Mr. Yamashiro all my life, but I had no idea what his first name was. Even his wife called him Mr. Yamashiro.

We shuffled through all the papers, an incredible number of papers for one simple thing. Mr. Yamashiro glanced up at the clock every so often, as I did. He was becoming almost as good as I was at pretending not to wait for Ivan.

Finally he asked, "And Ivan?"

I shook my head no.

"Ah." He nodded sympathetically.

Mr. Yamashiro got up and went over to the small refrigerator behind his desk and opened it. He pulled out two cold beers and took the tops off both.

He handed me a beer and waited for me to take a sip before he did. I thought it must be a hard business to stay sober in, and I was grateful for the beer.

He gave me copies of all the papers. I looked down at Ivan's drunken signature leaking all over the bottom of the page, rolled up his copy, and put it in the pocket of my coat.

I finished the beer and stood up. "If you don't need me for anything else?" I asked.

"No, no, everything's fine," Mr. Yamashiro said. He came around to my side of the desk and took my arm again, like I'd suddenly turned a hundred years old and couldn't walk on my own.

Then I changed my mind about leaving. It seemed as though someone should wait, should mark the time between the body of the boy we were giving and the ashes we were going to get back.

I sat back down again. "I wouldn't mind another beer," I said.

Mr. Yamashiro nodded, went around behind his desk, and opened up the refrigerator for two more beers.

While we drank the beer, Mr. Yamashiro talked about his papaya groves.

"It's the land that matters," he said. "It's an anchor. Otherwise we'd all be floating around . . . like Ivan," he ventured.

I nodded.

"We'd be doing rash things, like moving to the Mainland," he added.

"Yes," I agreed.

He shrugged. "Trying on new lives, like clothes on a rack."

I agreed.

Mr. Yamashiro had another appointment, so when we finished the second beer, he locked the door to his office, shook my hand, and motioned for me to wait on the padded bench in the hallway outside. That was another thing about the business end of death, all the padded surfaces, neutral-colored, as if a bright color sneaking in would somehow remind people what they were doing there in the first place.

On the bench, I watched a man coming out of the workroom, pulling off large gloves. He looked up and down the hall, then motioned me into a larger room where there was a full-sized refrigerator and a kitchen table with comfortable chairs around it. It was where they waited, he told me, between jobs.

There was food on the table, a few plates of okazu, and he offered me some but I couldn't eat. All the food looked like body parts. The fishcake looked like slices of brain and the cone sushi was as wrinkled and misshapen as a drowned body. I did take another beer.

Outside, the rain picked up, and the dark api leaves slapped against the windows.

The man asked if I wanted to watch the burning of the body.

"Sure," I said, certain he was joking.

A few minutes later I found myself staring through an unplugged hole in the oven wall. All I could see was a wall of flame.

"You see it?" he asked.

I nodded, as if I were seeing something besides fire.

I was about to step away from the hole when I saw the body. Saw it buckle, and then the arms rising up in some kind of embrace of heat and fire, as if he were still waving at the boat in Hilo Bay.

I jumped straight back away from the oven and ran out of the room and down the tiled hallway and out the front door before I even knew what I was doing. I went past the truck and kept running, with Nicholas's flaming arms still in front of my face.

The streets were wet and as I ran my slippers flipped water and mud up the back of my legs, and I took off my slippers and kept running downhill towards the water.

The harbormaster took one look at my face and pulled me into his office and sat me down. I kept my back to the pier so I wouldn't have to see any boats, and as I caught my breath I told him what I'd seen at the crematorium.

"Shit, Kinau, you had no business going in that room."

"I want a beer," I said.

"I can't drink in here, that's the rules."

"I know that," I said.

He leaned under the desk and pulled out a bottle and a glass and poured me a whiskey.

"Where the hell is Ivan?"

I shrugged and took a sip of the drink.

"Shit, Kinau."

"You're telling me."

"Listen, Alapai's down here helping his buddy put a boat in drydock. I'll tell him to come up here afterwards, okay?"

I nodded.

By the time Alapai appeared we'd made quite a dent in the bottle. He put his hand on my shoulder and squeezed until it hurt, like we used to do when we were kids testing each other. I was ignoring the pain, so Alapai let go of my shoulder and pulled up a chair and the harbormaster set out another shot glass.

I was good and mad at Ivan, and they agreed with everything I said because I was getting drunk and that's how you deal with drunk people, you just nod yes. Agree with everything. I would have felt better if they'd argued with me, because to have everyone suddenly agreeing with you is to become the loneliest person on earth.

Alapai started talking about fishing, and then about a time in Japan when heavy rain flooded the moat around the Imperial Palace in Tokyo. The royal carp swam out of the moat and into the gutters throughout the city, and all the people ran up and down the streets catching the fish in nets, handbags, even with their bare hands. Can you imagine what that must feel like, Alapai said, to hold a fish that's over a hundred years old in your hands.

For a second time, I saw Nicholas's arms rising in the heat.

The harbormaster said he'd caught salmon that had fallen apart in his hands, just disintegrated.

I saw his body buckle and his head come up, and I reached for the bottle and poured another shot. My mother used to say that the worst things you ever see, no matter how terrible at the time, turn out to be windows looking out on something else. Sometimes my mother was full of shit, I thought.

Nothing you can do about salmon that old, the harbormaster was saying. Next year's fish food.

Or bears, Alapai said. The bears come in and it's as easy as grocery shopping, throwing salmon into a grocery cart. But the Japanese, he said, carried all the carp back to the palace.

I asked what the point was, suddenly tired of hearing about fish.

The point, Alapai said, was that the people gave all the fish back.

So what, I said.

He told me I needed to give the boy back, whether they wanted him or not. He made it clear that he wasn't just talking about the boy.

21

*T*hat night, Ivan called with his excuses why he hadn't been at the crematorium. He'd gotten the time wrong, he said, and then asked how it went.

"How do you think it went, Ivan?"

"Listen, I'm sorry. I did mean to make it."

"Well. Nicholas's ashes are still with Mr. Yamashiro."

"Right. I didn't think you'd take them with you," he said.

"No," I said. "I didn't."

He offered to come up and spend the night, but I

thought it was better that he stay where he was. I told him I'd be down in Hilo tomorrow with flower deliveries, and we hung up.

I picked up the brush Ivan had used on my skin. It was my mother's hairbrush, given to her by one of her husbands, I didn't know which.

As far as men went, my mother hadn't done any better than I had, she'd just done it far more often. But she was never as cheerful as when she could see the end of a marriage coming. She brushed her hair a hundred licks every night, dressed in her oldest muumuus, turned on the stereo, and sang along with her operas, all that bloodthirsty music pouring through the house. She sliced out the chunks of worn lauhala matting and took new leaves from the lauhala tree outside and carefully cut the thorns off and soaked the long leaves until they were pliable and fed them into the mat.

That's how it was when my father decided to move back to the Mainland, with opera pouring through the house, my mother on her knees reweaving the lauhala. When I was little, Alapai's mother told me that the Mainland swallowed men whole. She said that the Mainland was such a hussy, such a wrecker of men.

The day my father was to leave for the Mainland, my mother and I woke up early and drove up the hill to pick the white ginger that grew in thick rows on either side of the road. It was my father's favorite flower and I was going to make him not one lei but three or four so he'd know how I felt about the Mainland swallowing him whole. I thought the flowers would give him luck, if he kept the leis, hung them up and let them dry out, as I'd done with every lei I'd ever been given.

The mist was so thick that we couldn't see much farther than each other and the white flowers directly in front of us. My mother was humming a favorite aria from Puccini, and above her humming I suddenly heard a dragging scratching noise like a trowel scraping concrete. I closed my eyes and listened.

It turned out to be a dog, pulling itself slowly down the road towards us.

My mother looked at it and said, "Rabies."

"No such thing," I said. "Not here." I'd learned that at school. No rabies in Hawaii.

"That so? Well, what are you going to call it then, if you can't call it rabies?"

The dog was still pushing itself towards us, and I felt like running in the opposite direction. Even the 'ohi'a trees were shuddering to get away from the dog. A beard of foam dangled from its chin, like a piece of Pele's hair caught on a branch.

"An accident? Maybe it was hurt by a car."

She sighed heavily. "Get my gun."

She was always telling me to get her gun. A day didn't go by without something making her angry enough to shoot at it. Politicians' signs, Hawaii Visitor Bureau signs, developers' signs. My father tried to make her actions seem normal. Once, on our way out to a fancy dinner to celebrate a good report card I'd gotten, she suddenly pulled her car over on the side of a road, got out and shot holes in a hotel sign saying Private Beach, and then unloaded the gun and dumped it back into the trunk, smoothed down her dress, and got back into the car and drove off down the road. My father leaned over into the back-seat and winked at me. "Everyone's got their little quirks," he said, "and we sure are proud of that report card," as my mother tore off towards Hilo.

"Get the gun," she repeated.

I went around to the back of her Nash and banged hard on the trunk to pop it open. Guns, knives, blankets, soil samples, cans of Spam, old telephone books for toilet paper. Anything you'd need for a state of disaster or a shipping strike on the Mainland. She even had C rations. The military was the biggest business in Hawaii, so everyone had C rations, but none of us would be caught dead actually eating the stuff. I thought we were all saving it up for the next war, something to feed the enemy.

"There's never been a case of rabies here," I said, handing her the gun.

She rolled her eyes upwards. "Spare me the child's opinion."

The dog was coming closer, about halfway across the road. I didn't like how it looked, either, but not enough to kill it.

"You forgot my hat."

I went back to the car and banged on the trunk again, and pulled out a funny little cap that looked like something a golf pro would wear. She swore it brought her good luck. In her muumuu and her plaid hat and her gun, she looked to me like the one with rabies.

She swung her gun up and took the stance. I closed my eyes and listened for cars, but she'd already made sure there weren't any.

She shot the dog right between the eyes, and it jumped backwards like a trick dog at the circus. Then it looked straight at us, not seeing anything at all, and crumpled over like an old coat.

She went over to the dog and prodded it with her foot. "Dead," she said.

Then she took aim and shot the dog again, and the already dead body shuddered and then spread out even flatter, this time like an oil slick.

"You kill something once to get it out of this life," she said, breaking down the gun, "and then you kill it again to keep it out of the next. It's like insurance," she said.

She took the ridiculous hat off and smoothed her long hair back off her face. Hunting always brought a certain radiance to her looks.

But her mind wasn't really on the dog at all that day. Perhaps she'd been aiming at a couple of ex-husbands. If you don't have your mind on the thing you're trying to get rid of, it will always circle around and come back to you.

I didn't have any of that figured out then. Children don't look into the future, the present is as much turmoil as they can handle. The dead dog was between thick green walls of ginger that were twice my height. On the ground were the two spent shells that my mother never picked up, because like most hunters she thought a bullet shell was somehow a decorative addition to the landscape.

I put the sack of ginger flowers in the trunk and sat in the car. I didn't want to pick any more ginger.

My mother came up to the window and knocked on the glass.

I tried to ignore her, but she swung the door open and handed me the shovel.

"You get to dig," she said brightly, as if it was something I'd be pleased by.

She picked up a back leg of the dog and dragged it through the ginger and into the forest. I followed with the shovel.

When we came to a small open space, she stopped. "We'll plant him here," she said. "Start digging."

It was a large dog, and I knew I'd be there for a long time.

My mother sat down on the trunk of a fallen koa tree, lit a cigarette, and started telling me about some of her ex-husbands.

I dug and listened and thought of my father at home, packing.

"It's the first one you miss the most," she said. "Probably because there's no one else to compare him with. My first was a bum, really, but I didn't see it at the time. All he wanted to do was fish. He'd stay out all day, then come home, have a few beers, and go to bed early so he could get up and go fishing the next day." I could feel her looking at me. "It's not a setup that can last very long."

She stood up and glanced at the hole, then at the dog. "You need to make it longer," she said.

I took off my sweatshirt, threw it on the grass, and kept digging. About halfway through digging the hole, I realized it was not a punishment. I don't know how I knew this, I just did. It takes years to make sense out of what you know.

"Still, I sometimes miss him. I sure got sick of eating fish, though." She shrugged, threw her cigarette down, and stomped on it. "Tell you what, I'll take you to meet him sometime. How's that sound?"

I thought it sounded terrible.

Another one was a gambler. "One week our bank account would be full of money, the next week I'd be bouncing checks. He's a mathematician, you know. That's what got him in the first place. Math." She shook her head. "I don't want to see you get good at math."

I sighed and kept digging. The ground was softer at the top, almost spongy, and harder deeper down.

"You always pick somebody exactly the opposite the second time. It's not until the third or fourth that you start figuring out what it is you're looking for, and it's not necessarily love."

I thought about the dog and that maybe it was lucky my father was going to the Mainland.

"I'm not digging anymore," I said, climbing out of the hole.

"Well, that's probably deep enough anyway." My mother dragged the dog over to the edge of the hole and rolled it in with her foot.

We stood on opposite sides of the hole, looking at the dog.

"Should we say something?" my mother asked, smiling at me.

I never knew what was going to put her in a good mood, though I supposed burying a dog could now be added to the list.

I shook my head. I'd already spoken to the dog, under my breath, so quiet that even the ʻohiʻa lehua trees couldn't hear, though they were leaning forward to catch each word. I'd wished the dog luck on his journey, and I told him I wouldn't forget where he'd been buried.

Later, when I circled my father's neck with ginger leis, it was a dead dog I was smelling.

22

_W_hen Hilo Bay behaved like something other than water, when it rose up on its hands and knees and crawled towards the town, everyone kept one eye on it. I looked down towards the water, registering the color. Blue-gray, moving towards gray, and still inching towards the town.

As I delivered flowers to the florists and plants to the shops, I noticed that the bounty was having a slow day, with only two sharks hanging under the eaves. After dropping off my final orders, I went into stores and shopped for things I didn't need, a new yukata kimono for summer, a dozen more candles, a small round Buddha because he had the same soft smile as Mr. Yamashiro did when he was thinking about his papaya groves.

On the street, I felt the bay crowding me, the air becoming more liquid. I turned my back to the water and walked up past the okazu shop, then cut over past the Kau-kau Drive-in, and for the first time in my life I didn't stop in even though it was the day they were serving kalua pig. The air was thick with the late-afternoon scent of runaway growth and rotted fruit heating in the sun, a smell almost sickeningly sweet.

I didn't want to think of Ivan. I thought about my knees, because they were aching, the way they did whenever I was nervous. I looked in all the windows, the small shops, the offices, the liquor store light blinking beer, beer, beer.

I didn't know what I was looking for, exactly; some woman in a red dress reflecting in the window like an answer, some version of myself? I looked at each window as the sun bounced off the glass, turning each pane into a mirror and then disappearing into the next.

What if the story of the shark-men went like this? What if it took years for the shark jaw to emerge from the skin? What if until then those shark-men went around changing lightbulbs and worrying about the oil in your car and the whole time their shark jaw was forming, those long gray teeth just waiting to burst through the skin?

The King of Love was sitting outside, wearing a turquoise cape, his battered crown, and a plumeria tucked behind one ear. He looked up when he saw me coming out of the tackle shop and patted a spot next to him on the bench.

"Hey," I said, sitting down.

He smiled, held his hands out, and turned them over. Age spots on one side, pale skin on the other. He'd once told me his hands were exactly like my mother's.

"Can I ask you something?" I said.

He looked surprised, then nodded at the water. "Look," he said, "Hilo Bay is showing off."

It was true. The bay preened and turned like a bird showing off first one color, then another. Dark navy with ripples of gold, and then when the clouds blew off, a light turquoise the color of fog glass, then patches of dark hunter green, the color of the bicycle that Alapai had for only one day. When the sun came through completely, the water became the loud oil-spill colors of mahimahi, a fish as flashy underwater as a peacock was above.

It was so close to something my mother would have done, to wait out a question until it dissolved into the air.

I laughed and he looked pleased.

We watched the bay a while longer, until the water was gray again, and the King of Love said he had to get home and I should, too.

But instead, I waited. Sat on the bench and listened to every sound in Hilo, from the trucks sighing their way up the steep hill past the library to the roaches rustling under the fallen leaves. To my own ridiculous heart going into overdrive every time someone walked past who was tall like Ivan, or had dark hair like Ivan, or swing his hips like Ivan.

There were two bars on the street, and I figured Ivan had to go into or come out of one eventually. I wouldn't go into the bars and look for him, I wouldn't make that much of a fool of myself. I wasn't that far gone. I pulled the Buddha out of the shopping bag and set it on the bench beside me.

In the liquor store, the posters were up for the Year of the Pig, which was always a lucky year. A fat happy pig pranced over the beer cooler, his fancy turquoise shirt straining at the buttons. I slid open the beer cooler and leaned down into the chilly air. After sitting on the bench, my hair was wet with sweat, my body clammy. I bought li hing mui, a dried sweet plum, along with a quart of cold beer. Six-packs were for regular consumption, but it was the Year of the Pig, and quarts were for comfort.

Outside the liquor store, a group of girls passed by, staring at me as unconsciously and acceptingly as girls that age do; I could be a dog with a broken leash trailing from my neck, I could be the King of Love with his cardboard crown.

Hilo held tight to its own, and so the King of Love was just any one of us, like the old woman who carried the doll, the local surfing champion, the winner of the annual anthurium contest. Hilo threw an arm out around the town and pulled everyone in. What it did to us in that embrace might be another matter, but that wasn't the point.

I drank cold beer on the bench with the Buddha smiling beside me and I ate the salty dried plum and watched the leaves move and figured I'd probably missed Ivan while I was in the liquor store and that might have been what I wanted.

A light went on in a second-story window across the street. There was a sound of girls giggling for a few minutes and then a sudden quiet, their laughter replaced by a hula teacher tuning her ukulele and gently bossing the class into order.

Gradually the shops along the street closed for the evening and the tops of the trees drew away into the darkness, until finally the only illumination was the window floating above the liquor store.

The window was too high for me to see inside the room, so I stood up on the edge of the bench and leaned across the branch of a plumeria tree, spilling the white sap over my hands. Even standing on the bench all I could see was their hands when they raised them overhead, beautiful young hands clustering around the lightbulb like dark winged moths.

I held out my sticky hands. I'd never looked that closely at them since hula class. I thought of my hands on Ivan's back. His waist. My hands touching his face, that first night he came back, how even the skin could lie.

The class started out with Green Rose Hula, the teacher's voice smooth and melodious. She came over to the window to catch the evening breeze. It was too dark outside for her to see me, though I could see her clearly, a large woman holding her ukulele high above her breasts.

As she sang, I danced hula along with them. My feet moved okay, but my hands were useless. Whenever the class stopped I couldn't shake the feeling that it was because of my own mistakes.

Aina mai ana kapuana, the woman sang, over and over. Here is the story. The repetition of it suddenly made sense to me. Who ever caught the whole story the first time around? It was the same way that my mother gave advice. She just repeated herself over and over again, and when I hit a certain age it made sense. *Aina mai ana kapuana.* Some lights don't turn on until you're tall enough to reach them.

As I danced, I thought of the greenhouses, that when I was a child being there wasn't work, they were different, magical places, and except for Volcano, the only place on earth where I saw my mother truly at ease in the world. Long cool tunnels of leaves the size of houses, the damp cement under my running feet, the sighing of the sprinklers overhead, the sharp smell of turned soil. My mother leaning over me, smelling as clean as a freshly crushed leaf, explaining which plants were indigenous and which weren't. You could ruin an entire forest with one wrong seed, she told me. It was important to get rid of what didn't belong before it took over, she said, a theory she applied to people as well.

Then I heard the end of the hula. Over and over, *aina mai ana kapuana.* My mother had drowned in Hilo Bay, along with others from the town, her body gaffed up by death-weary fishermen. Her long white hair had grown during her week underwater, and her skin had taken on the cast of pale green seaweed. To see someone who'd drowned changed the faces of everyone still living.

I had my mother's body cremated, and then Alapai and I took her ashes out to sea, just beyond Hilo Bay. I opened the small metal canister and held it up into the wind. Nothing happened. Her ashes hadn't scattered like sand, or gravel, the way I thought they were supposed to. Her ashes fell over the side of the boat in a fist-shaped clump that splashed as it hit the surface of the water and sank, and Alapai laughed and said we shouldn't expect my mother to do things in the usual way. But when I saw that clump of ash, I realized that I'd spread her ashes in the wrong place. It should have been up the mountain in Volcano, where her ashes could have blown over the thick ferns, up into the 'ohi'a trees like mist, like smoke, like a mother.

Across the street, the front door to a bar opened, and then slammed shut. I heard his voice and leaned back on the bench, halfway into the bushes.

Ivan. He was standing just outside the circle of light, talking to a woman and running his hands through his hair the way he did when he wanted to be looked at. I couldn't see much of the woman, just a general outline. He'll take her swimming, I thought. He'd devour her. He'll wish for a jaw in his back, but he was only a man. I wondered how much beer I'd had.

They stopped talking and none of us moved. Then he bent down and cupped her face in his hand.

I couldn't believe I could be so quiet, watching that. I watched her lean closer until it looked like he was the only thing holding her up.

They crossed the street, walking straight towards me, I couldn't believe they didn't see me. I pushed farther back into the bushes. The light swarmed around their heads as they stepped into and out of the shoplights.

Then the woman turned in my direction and I caught a glimpse of her sorrowful face, and it was one I'd always know, no matter how much time had passed. Victoria.

23

*I*n the motel, I was still hearing Ivan's voice over the phone earlier in the day, a stranger's voice explaining someone else's life. He said he couldn't come to my house anymore, that Victoria knew he'd spent time with me. He said she was vulnerable and this wasn't the time to tell her about us.

I held the phone to my ear. "I saw her, you know."

"Where?"

"With you. Downtown, last night."

He paused, and I thought of her face.

"What were you doing there?" he asked.

"I live here, Ivan, remember?"

Even so, I told myself this was a second chance. And then I asked what I shouldn't have. "Why is she here?"

"She felt it necessary."

What the hell does that mean, I thought, but I didn't ask. I told myself that Victoria was just here for her son's ashes, nothing more.

In the motel, I wrapped a maile lei around me like a sash. I'd brought it with me because I wanted it to be perfect, I wanted the scent of the maile leaves to remind him of the greenhouses.

It didn't make me think of the greenhouses, though. It made me think of my mother's long hair and how it floated around her when she swam in the stream behind our house, her long hair loose in the water, then as she stepped up out of the water, her hair wrapped tight against her skin.

Because Ivan was late, I stood in front of the motel mirror, brushed my hair, unbuttoned my blouse, stared at my breasts, buttoned my blouse back up, brushed my hair again, sat down, and stood up. I pretended to be someone else, not a hard thing to do under the circumstances.

I opened the bottle of wine I'd brought and watched the woman in the motel mirror drink a glass. The shadows crawled across the room like a fungus, and I picked up the phone to make sure it was in order.

I ran my hand over my skin the way I thought he would, my hand almost becoming his hand, my skin soft, eager.

A cockroach crawled across the bathroom shelf. I blew on it and it disappeared and then the feelers stuck back up above the shell with the small wrapped square of soap, and I reminded myself that life was good, a treasure.

While waiting, I watched television. A program on sharks played over and over on the cable channel, I nearly had it memorized, how the two sharks swam together, down into the reef and back up to the surface, their movements almost in tandem, and then one of the sharks swam too close to a coral-head, somehow scraped itself, and the other shark turned on it so suddenly that it took my breath away, each time. And then a moment later the screen was filled with even more sharks ripping into the belly of the wounded shark, pulling loose the intestines and swimming off with them clamped in their jaws, small clouds of blood released into the water, puffs of blood opening like Japanese paper flowers in water, and I had the paranoid idea that Victoria's money was somehow keeping this shark documentary on the television, as an excuse for continuing the bounty and we'd all be forced to witness it and watch it on TV forever.

I turned the television off and read the time from a clock screwed into the wall. I was suddenly furious to be stuck in this depressing room because Ivan said he couldn't come to my home anymore, because he hadn't told Victoria about us. I was even more furious to find myself so vulnerable.

I packed up my things, and left the lei. I was putting everything into the truck when Ivan pulled up in the parking space next to mine. I looked at the clock on my dashboard and not his face.

"Good," he said, getting out of his car. "You have the key?"

"I'm not going back in there."

He walked to the door of the motel room, stuck his head in, and turned back to me.

"It's okay," he said. "We can go in now." Like he'd chased the boogeymen from under the bed. "Listen, I can't stay long," he said, looking at his watch.

I shook my head no, but his hands were on me.

"My being late, right? That's got you upset? I couldn't get away."

"You're lying," I said.

"Come," he said softly, taking my hand. "Please come."

Next to us, a couple packing up a car glanced at us curiously. The woman paused a moment, the way women do when they're trying to see if you're all right.

"There's a maile lei in that room."

"I don't like what you're doing, Ivan."

"What am I doing? You think I have everything figured out, Kinau? You think I'm less confused than you are?"

"What is Victoria doing here?"

He leaned against the door of the truck. With his finger, he outlined my mouth. "When you're upset, or when you don't feel well, you get a white ring around your mouth. Did you know that?"

I was still angry, I was keeping the thought of it, but I could feel it leaving my body. He closed the door to the truck.

On the bed, the green maile leaves crackled around us like kindling. For Ivan, I thought, love and betrayal might be the same thing, a bite on the shoulder, a slap to the face, a woman becoming more vulnerable, more furious.

What I remembered was so different from what I was experiencing. I remembered him lifting up my long hair in his hand, his lips along the back of my neck, and from somewhere he had a plumeria flower in his hand and he tucked it behind my ear.

I remembered slipping into the shallow water of the stream behind my mother's house. We had three-pronged spears and flashlights to fish for opai, the prawns that showed their bright blue eyes in the light of the flashlight, and there was a moon out, a full moon that night, what was called hoku, and he followed me into the stream but then pretended to lose his balance and rocked forward and then backwards and I laughed as he went under the surface of the water and swam over to me in the dark and grabbed hold of my legs and I knew he was going to do it but I screamed anyway and he pulled me underwater with him, in the cold stream, and found my mouth as I felt his hands slipping under my clothes, peeling off my wet shirt in the stream.

It was what I remembered.

Yet this was something different, wrestling, a struggle to fit this Ivan together with the one I remembered. It was like weaving old rope into new, what you wound up with was always weaker.

Ivan had to leave almost immediately to be back in Hilo to meet Victoria, and he left before I did.

I drove back along the Hamakua coast, where the cliffs were full of small caves, and I started thinking of how the caves had been formed, what I always thought of as the for-no-reason stories to do with Pele, the goddess of the volcano. Like my mother, Pele was always getting huhū at someone, all worked up, only she used lava the way my mother used her guns; as retribution, as warning, sometimes as sport. Pele was angry once, for no reason, and sent a path of burning lava down the hillside, through a forest of 'ohi'a lehua trees. The lava ran all the way down to the sea, which opened its wet mouth and lapped up the hot lava and burnt its tongue and the walls of its mouth and that's why there are caves along the seashore, from Pele getting angry one day for no reason.

It made good sense to me. There was always a reason.

On the bayfront, the King of Love was moving slowly towards the harbor. There were so many things I wanted to ask him, but mostly I just felt like yelling. I rolled down the window and stopped the truck.

He turned on me with such a look that I knew he'd been harassed recently, probably by high school kids, and for a moment I felt we were wearing the same face.

"How's it going?" I asked.

"The King of Love is doing less than perfect, but better than some," he said, composing himself. He handed me a helium balloon, and as I took it I thought that like all kings, he talked about himself in the third person.

"You seem a little anxious," he said, when I pulled the truck over and got out.

I nodded.

Several cars passed, and the King of Love waved to them.

"What do you think," I said, finally, "about trying to bring back the past?"

"The past," he said. "You left your balloon in the truck," he said. "You know, helium only lasts a short time. Couple of hours at most." A car slowed down and the King of Love stepped out into the street and handed a balloon through the window.

I tried again. "What I mean is, when your feelings are going one way and your thoughts another?"

He smiled, coming back to the curb. "I take a nap."

"Ah," I said.

"It doesn't help much, but then again it doesn't do any harm."

I drove home with the balloon bumping the ceiling of my truck, remembering that Alapai had once told me that the King of Love was there like the Red Cross, not to avert disaster, but to remind you that the next one was just around the corner.

24

*W*hat pay phone are you calling from?" I asked, listening to the early-morning sounds behind Ivan's voice. I heard a delivery truck, what sounded like crates of milk being unloaded onto a sidewalk, the birds roosting in the trees with the sound of paper crumpled in a fist.

I pictured him slipping out of his hotel room, telling Victoria he was going for a newspaper, or down to the bakery for hot malasadas. This early the streets in Hilo would still be wet from the night rains, and the sunlight would bounce off the street right up into your eyes, and there probably wasn't another person in the whole town using a pay phone.

"I'm in front of that okazu shop,"he said.

My life was clear to everyone, in fact it was this week's headline. Everyone knew that while he was officially staying at the hotel down in Hilo, Ivan had spent his nights with me up the mountain. And then when Victoria showed up and that time was officially over and we went to motels during the day, I could tell that people knew that as well, by the way they averted their eyes when I bought something at the store, when I stood in line at the post office.

Alapai told me that people were saying I couldn't get over Ivan because my family had ended, my mother dying in the tsunami, my father dying on the Mainland. I could have turned into a criminal and the town would have forgiven me because my mother was one of the many who'd died in the tsunami and it was said that people who lived through it were marked by it. There was a watermark on our skin, a different amount of liquid floating around in our brains, and from that time on we lived in a world that wasn't wet or dry, but somewhere in between. It just sounded like Hilo, to me.

They said that was why I could not let go of Ivan, because I met him when I still believed my mother was alive. But in the long run some things are unexplainable and it doesn't help to chase after them, searching for clues.

I was having an affair with my ex-husband, they all said, with a shake of the head, a go-figure shrug of the shoulders, hands thrown out in front of them as if their lives were as clean as the air between their palms.

I listened to Ivan's voice, so easy over the telephone, just wanting to say good morning. That was all, nothing else.

After I hung up the phone, I stepped on the helium balloon, trying to pop it. I remembered that last night I had dreamed of quick movement, of darting from object to object, swimming effortlessly, moving through the water as if it were air, then diving down deep along the reef as small clouds of fish scattered like confetti in front of me, then turned and swam parallel to the reef. It wasn't until I woke that I realized I was swimming not as a human but as a shark.

Who comes through a love affair intact?

What had happened to the Hawaiian girl who was impregnated by the shark god? How did she feel after her baby swam away for good? Did she marry, try to have a regular life? Was it even possible to go back to the dry bed of a human? Did she hold her breath as each of her children was born,

and find herself secretly disappointed that they had
no fins, no jaw in their backs, no special agility in
the water? Did regret beat against her skin like
small fists, her thoughts running underwater, small
waves whispering what if, what if?

Every version of the Hawaiian girl's story ended
with her putting the baby to sea. Why is it that
what we need to hear most is always the part left
out of the story? Alapai's tutu would have said that
we make up only as much as we need right then.

So here's what happened next: She moved far
away from her parents' house, all the way to the
leeward side of the island. She went far inland. That
way, the sea couldn't haunt her, and the shark god
would have trouble finding her, slipping into her
dreams again.

She joined a new community, and grew wetland
taro. She was friendly, but mostly kept to herself.
Then one day, while knee-deep in mud and plant-
ing a row of taro, she saw a reflection in the water
pooled in the surface of the mud, and her heart
swept side to side like a poorly moored boat, water
slapping her ribs, the ends of her long hair dipping
into the water.

Whose face was it? I didn't know yet.

25

On the pier, the men involved in the bounty moved back and forth, some carrying their importance in the small of their backs, others in the swagger of their legs or the quick movements of their hands, wrists cocked, fingers loosely splayed.

A hierarchy had been established, from the person who measured the length of each shark, to the man who wrote the figure down in a little book and multiplied it by whatever price Ivan was paying this day, down to the man who had the job of gutting each shark. I had no idea how this man had been selected. He was a truck gardener who brought his produce into Hilo several times a week and drove up and down the streets selling won bok and fresh ginger out of the back of it. I'd never seen this man near a boat, though I recognized his new prestige in the way he shuffled in his fake-leather slippers with the small toes hanging out each side. Still, he was good, and held the knife in a crowd-pleasing way, thumb out. Each time he opened a shark and ripped slowly down its belly, his knife making a tearing sound in the flesh like a piece of strong canvas ripping, the crowd went on automatic pilot and collectively held its breath, while buoys and beer cans and even plastic bottles of bleach spilled out with the stomach. Mostly people were just curious, wondering at everything the shark had swallowed.

On the dock, all the men were dry from the waist up. Each man was circled by a crowd, and though I was too far away to hear, I watched their hands telling the same story that every other pair of hands had been telling since the beginning of the bounty. How many, how big, what kind of fight it put up, what else was caught on the trip.

A new boat came in, moments after the first, and the center changed as the crowd broke apart and moved down the pier to where that boat was moored. It seemed like the only thing missing was a shave-ice stand. The sharks were dead, but everything else felt brand-new, and oddly festive. People walked carefully through the blood on the sidewalks, the women pulling up their muumuus slightly, and kids on bicycles rode through the blood with their feet held out to the sides, and were scolded for it and then immediately forgiven.

Rival shopkeepers came out from behind their cash registers, squatted on the sidewalk, and nodded over the same dead shark. People moved chairs outside their offices and conducted business in their doorways, every dog in town was down at the harbor barking as the boats came in, and all the bars were full of fishermen who suddenly found themselves more important and a little richer than they'd been before. They weren't just fishing, they were in some way saving something, making the waters safe, even for haole boys from the Mainland.

Of course, there were those who saw the bounty as a massive slaughter and shook their heads in disgust, and wrote letters to the newspaper, and they compared the bounty to a witch-hunt—but those weren't the people in the bars buying rounds with Ivan's money.

26

Over breakfast, I was trying to interest a client from the Mainland in anthuriums. I told her that they shipped better than most of my other flowers, and held up longer once they got to the Mainland, but the truth was I had a greenhouse full of them that I needed to move, or find myself another line of work. The business of flowers wasn't like the business of plants. Plants could wait, grow larger, and make more money in the long run. Flowers were for gamblers, risk-takers. I was trying to stay light and cheerful, because if she knew I had flowers to move and no other buyer, she'd offer me nothing for them.

There was a change in temperature, a sudden kona wind, and outside the window the light rain stopped as abruptly as it had begun.

In the middle of the conversation Ivan came into the restaurant with Victoria. I went hot and cold and would have bolted from the room except for the fact that they were being seated by the door. He should know I am here, I thought, he should sense my presence, but he just smiled at the waitress and pulled a chair out for Victoria and then sat down across from her.

I nodded at my client, ordered the same food she did, ate it without tasting it, the whole time with one eye on Ivan and Victoria, my heart beating all the way down into my hands.

Victoria was thinner than I remembered, with almost girlish mannerisms, her hands continually touching her face, then touching his arm like a blind person reassuring herself. I'd like to say I didn't count how many times she touched him, but I did.

My client asked if it was true that the Chinese especially liked the anthuriums.

"Absolutely," I said. I would have agreed with anything. I asked if she knew what people called anthuriums. Boy flowers, I told her, because of the stamen sticking out. She thought that was delightful. The boy flower got them every time. I didn't even want to understand why.

"Do you think it's true that different races prefer different flowers?"

"Oh, sure," I said.

"Such as?"

She looked more interested than she had all morning. "Well, let's see, you're right about the Chinese and anthuriums." I watched Victoria place her hand on the table and Ivan's hand then cover it.

"So, the Chinese," I said, watching Ivan's hand, "they also like lilies, especially amaryllis."

She nodded. "What about the Japanese?"

"They like orchids," I said, "flowers that are hard to take care of and require patience."

"Really?" she said.

Victoria smiled at Ivan.

"Now, Hawaiians," I said, "like flowers they can wear, that smell good. Those are my favorite, as well." I thought of the maile lei I'd taken to the motel the other day.

She nodded encouragingly. "That's so interesting. What about white people?"

"Most haoles want potted plants, flowers they don't have to take care of. They'll buy a plant like a chrysanthemum, because they know it'll live longer than other flowers, even without watering. They can take it home, stick it on a table, and forget it."

She laughed.

Victoria touched Ivan's face briefly, and I thought that he hadn't told her anything about us, or she would never touch him like that.

"Then there are the hotels," I said. "They don't care what flowers they get, as long as they're big and showy, plants the size of furniture, birds-of-paradise with leaves longer than a woman's torso, blossoms larger than a face . . ." I trailed off.

When Ivan finally saw me, Victoria must have read his expression, because she turned to look as well. I shifted behind the plants separating the tables so they couldn't see me at all, and came back into the conversation, which had gotten back to anthuriums. When I looked again, they were leaving.

"Who are those people you've been watching?" my client asked, turning around.

I told her it was my ex-husband. I didn't tell her that Victoria was his wife.

She said, "Ah, the one who started the shark bounty?"

I nodded yes.

When the waiter came back, she ordered mimosas and we drank without saying much. I knew I was getting some kind of sympathy vote but I didn't care.

I wrapped up the sale and left the restaurant. In the parking lot, Ivan was leaning against my truck.

"Get lost," I said, unlocking the door.

He grabbed my wrist. "I'm sorry that happened," he said, nodding his head toward the restaurant.

"Me too," I said. "Let go of my arm."

"What were you doing in there, anyway?"

"Eating breakfast," I said.

"But why here?"

"I was invited, Ivan. My client is staying here."

"Promise me something," he said. "I want to go up to the volcano."

I just looked at him. Sometimes Ivan was unbelievable, beyond words.

"So, go."

"With you."

"Where's Victoria?"

"Resting. We'd just gone for Nicholas's ashes and she's exhausted."

I looked at his mouth. Ivan had one of those mouths that people looked at.

"How about it?" he asked.

I couldn't believe his nerve, but at the same time I was curious, wondering what he'd do next. So I agreed to go up to the volcano.

Before my father left for the Mainland, he'd brought me up to Kilauea and we'd watched an eruption together. I was sure the volcanic eruption had something to do with my father leaving, that all the new land would form in the wake he left behind, lava spilling all the way across the ocean to the Mainland. A bridge of new land for my father to run across. I figured the Mainland was somewhere off Kauai.

He told me that he and my mother were divorcing, that he was moving away but he'd be back to see me.

You can tell children anything but you can't count on them swallowing it. At the time, I believed my father had broken a sacred kapu, some rule set down by the ali'i, those in charge. I thought he had to go to the Mainland for refuge. I was certain there was a place on the Mainland like the City of Refuge over on the other side of the island, in Kona. In the old days, people who'd done something wrong could take off running for the City of Refuge, and if they made it, they were safe, no matter what they'd done. I thought the Mainland was full of people who'd done something wrong and had to run for their lives and that's where they'd wound up. I pictured my father's long feet running over the fields of lava, crumbly a'a lava that tore off his skin in chunks. My father's feet dancing over the thorns of the kiawe trees that were introduced by a French priest with a sense of humor, because who'd plant thorny kiawe on purpose? I thought the land was there to show you what you looked like—gutted and with your insides spread out—as you ran through it and the City of Refuge beckoned.

My father talked about coming back for visits, but why would he leave the City of Refuge once he'd made it there?

I thought I'd seen Pele that day. I saw a blue vapor rising up in the middle of the molten lava. The vapor took on the outline of a woman who appeared and disappeared, the way something does if you stare at it long enough.

Then I worried that the blue woman was showing up because someone had made an offering to Pele, maybe a pig, or some taro. But all I saw was people standing at the edge of the volcano for as long as they could take the fumes of the sulfur and the heat. Not seeing an offering worried me. What if it was my father making the offering? His hands were empty. What could he be offering but me?

Even up in Volcano the mist was shark-colored, and caught on the branches of the 'ohi'a trees. I parked at the observatory and we stepped out of the truck and into a thick mist. It was said that Pele sometimes traveled with a small dog, but there were no dogs among the people milling about at the guardrail, or looking through the telescopes at the view of shifting clouds.

After a moment the mist lifted and part of Kilauea became visible. Ivan said how much he'd missed seeing the volcano, that there was nothing comparable on the Mainland. He said some of his best memories were of us, sitting right here looking out at Kilauea. As he spoke, the mist covered the view again and the air around us became wet and heavy.

It wasn't Kilauea itself that made me nervous, I decided, it was the people I came here with. We waited for another glimpse of Kilauea, while around us the crowds surged and then disappeared. Finally Ivan said it was time for him to go. We were walking back to the truck when I saw him bend down quickly and pick up a piece of pahoehoe lava. He looked around at me and I pretended I hadn't seen him slip it into his pocket. Taking lava was bad luck and he knew it.

We left the volcano with that piece of lava still in his pocket. I didn't trust him. A man who stole lava, who deliberately took that kind of risk, was asking for his life to be changed for him, rather than changing it himself. I felt something new towards Ivan, and it was disappointment.

I didn't know why Ivan was stealing it, why rather than offering he was taking.

Because of the lava, I was certain we'd get in a car crash on the way home. Stealing lava from the volcano brought that kind of bad luck upon you. Nerve-wrecking bad luck.

Yet we made it back to Ivan's hotel without incident. After dropping him off, I drove down near the harbor and parked. I was hoping to find Alapai, that he would make me feel calmer, but I couldn't locate him in the crowd.

At the harbor the King of Love wasn't handing out balloons and plumerias on his usual corner. He wasn't carrying his megaphone. He walked along the pier, glaring at everyone, and when he came down to the edge of the water, he strode under the row of dead sharks, shaking his fist.

I was surprised at the size of the crowd. When the bounty was first announced, each fisherman had wanted to kill that first shark, the one that had attacked the boy. The boy belonged to everyone now, even if the sorrow everyone felt was mostly borrowed, as sorrow always is when a crowd picks it up and makes it theirs. The crowd milled around the sharks, and when I ran into the harbormaster, I asked him why there were so many people.

"Because Ivan, the fool . . ." He paused, looking embarrassed. "Excuse me, eh, Kinau? But he keeps raising prices. He's got plenty fishermen out there right now, but he keeps jacking the price up and then word gets out. We got a mob out there. And this is payday."

"Payday," I repeated. The fishermen were lined up, comparing shark lengths and patting each other on the back. They were all making fun of one man who was loudly claiming to have caught the largest shark, because it was known that he'd only caught three small ones. But not, he said, when you added them all together.

At the front of the line was a man behind a cardboard table, with an open fishing-tackle box, and the truck gardener, who'd been doing most of the tallying, stood with a small notebook in his hands, reading off names or numbers of sharks and their lengths. The men signed receipts for the money.

"It's not Ivan's money we're talking about, is it?" the harbormaster asked. "No one should throw his money around like that."

"Where would Ivan get money like that?" I said, and we both laughed. "It's hers."

He looked relieved. "I was beginning to think Ivan was getting pupule, you know?" He made a circle around his ear that meant crazy, then shrugged. It could be explained. It was someone from the Mainland.

27

Captain Cook came back twice during the Makahiki time, and that was where he went wrong. His second appearance wasn't predicted by the priests or even wanted. His boat didn't look so majestic this time, just a boat with tired sails, not angel's wings, the wooden hull croaking like a frog with sore joints.

People had tired of him, and the warriors, who'd always doubted that he was the god Lono, stepped onto center stage.

Cook came forward with the same bright expectations as he'd had the last time, when he was revered, worshiped.

But times change, people grow suspicious, what was once loved is cast away before it can open your heart a second time. Betrayal is only an arm's length away from love.

During his second appearance Cook was killed, on the shore by Kealakekua Bay, his body cut into pieces and eaten, saved, or given back to his men, depending on which version you chose to believe.

There was a monument marking the place of his death. I went down to the shoreline where it had happened and tried to imagine how it had felt for him, first to think of yourself as exactly what someone wanted, an answer, a beloved god, and then to watch the people grow tired of you and bring you down to earth.

Yet he must have had a sense that for just a moment he was truly invincible, that short sweet time before everything came together, the sky rushing down, the horizon moving up, two huge hands clapping down on the inconsequential. The point is, was it worth it?

Why didn't he leave? He'd come, done enough damage, and so why didn't he leave?

wind coming down the cliffs, the lava rushing through the ʻohiʻa lehua forests, Pele's sister running through the ironwood trees to get away from Pele's anger, and the destruction that followed her everywhere.

But Ivan didn't have to carry around a piece of stolen lava to know that all lives are filled with bad luck. Call it what you want. Call it opportunity.

Then Kilauea erupted. The lava flow poured down the mountain toward a subdivision that was less than five years old. People hurried to evacuate, took what they could with them while the lava pushed towards their neighborhoods. In the slow forward crunch, first the trees caught fire and turned black, then the wooden houses burned and disappeared. There was nothing left except an occasional car, the paint burned off, windows shattered. Just dark gray metal shapes parked in a field of lava, like mastodons caught in a tar pit. After the lava cooled, some people refused to go back and look at what was left.

Ivan was carrying the lava, and it made me feel the way I had after my mother died, that it was my fault, that I could have done something to change the course of events and I didn't. I imagined Ivan's hand on the lava, like a rabbit's foot caught on fire. A pain in the palm of his hand.

Still, I agreed to meet him in a motel just outside

28

When you carry a piece of lava, you expect bad luck to follow, and it does. After Ivan took the ropy pahoehoe lava from the volcano, there was a heavy rain that wouldn't stop. Boulders came loose and fell off the cliffs and blocked the roads. Fishing nets came up empty, with huge holes torn through them. A neighbor ran over his dog while trying to push his truck out of the mud.

On one hand it was just lava, a ropy curl of pahoehoe. On the other it was the whole Big Island, not just Kilauea, where the lava was from, but the

Kamuela, a small hollow tile room under the euca-
lyptus trees. This time I didn't get undressed, I
didn't bring a maile lei.

When Ivan came into the room, I could see he
was surprised.

"So here we are," he said, glancing around the
room.

"Yes."

"I passed a fruit stand on the way," he said, "and
I bought mangos." He reached into the bag he was
carrying, pulled out a mango, and set it on the
dresser. "I bought a lot," he said. "Past training.
Nicholas loved mangos. . . ."

"Oh?"

"Yeah, I used to buy mangos by the case, have
them shipped in. He'd go through the whole case in
a couple of days, make himself sick every time. Typ-
ical kid." He smiled, and shook his head.

"I liked his tattoo," I said.

"What?"

"The tattoo on his arm, it was such a great image,
the boat. Romantic, really."

"What tattoo?"

"Nicholas's. He had a clipper ship on his arm."

"He didn't have a tattoo," Ivan said, sharply.

"Yes, he did. He showed it to me."

"No," Ivan said, "he didn't."

I let it go, but thought of the anchor with no

name on it, the boy who'd come halfway around the world, whose hand was still too shy to touch an orchid.

I asked Ivan about us.

He looked uncomfortable. Perhaps I was like my mother, mistaking confrontation for commitment. "Well," he said, "there's not much I can do now, is there? I can't leave her now, I've got to wait."

He tried to hold me, but I pulled away from him.

"I'll go back to the Mainland with her, but I'll come back for trips, you know . . . and then I'll make the break."

"You're going back to the Mainland with her," I said, believing it and not believing it.

"It would just be for a while. Just to get her settled."

"Oh, right."

"I mean it."

"Ivan, don't lie to me."

"I'm not lying."

"No, you probably don't think you are." I opened the door and looked outside. I was suddenly tired. "Is this about her money? Is that what's going on?"

"No," he said, angry.

"Well, what is it?"

"I just can't. . . ."

"Well, I can't believe this is happening, all over again. You're leaving me, for the second time."

"No," he said, "I'm not."

"Listen to you, Ivan. You can't even convince yourself."

I stared out at the sun bouncing off my truck, a mynah bird slowly strutting across the parking lot.

"I'm not doing this anymore," I said.

29

*A*fter the girl gave away her shark baby, her
first tries with men didn't work. They splashed
through her taro fields, muddying the water, crush-
ing the plants with their large feet. Not realizing
who she was, they expected her to cook, and keep
house.

Then one night, the shark god came again. She
was working late in the fields, wading through the
rows of wetland taro. It was a full moon, which illu-
minated his manly shape. He dove right into the
water of her field and there was no splash, no sound

at all. She felt the water push against her legs and quickly subside. His dark shape swam towards her between the rows of taro, and the jaw in his back was visible in the moonlight.

Up close, a shark's jaw is a terrifying thing. Why hadn't she noticed this before?

She kept a kukui nut lamp burning this time. She would give her love to him as half of a flower, like the naupaka, which grows half of a flower up in the mountain, while the other half grows down at the seashore. So she saw her love for the shark god this way. As half of a flower.

When he came into the room where the kukui nut lamp was burning, he didn't bring the other half of the flower with him. His palms were open and floating in the darkness, and he was offering nothing, but nothing was something she already had plenty of, and she turned from him.

30

On the drive down to Hilo, I became more and more angry, drumming the steering wheel until my hand hurt. I drove along the sea road listening to the waves slapping, and came up on the pier where the boats were in a traffic jam and the fishermen were standing around the wet docks. I parked the truck and started yelling before I was even out of the cab.

"I don't care what the hell Ivan wants," I yelled, "the bounty's over."

I got a little closer. "I don't want to see any more sharks killed!" I shouted.

A few fishermen turned around and the crowd started looking at me but it wasn't until I pulled my gun out that they began hushing each other, that people started remembering who my mother was.

I climbed up on the hood of a truck. "It's over!" I yelled, so loud it hurt my throat. "It's over. No more money paid out for dead sharks. Go on home!"

No one moved, but someone in the crowd yelled that I was right.

I stomped on the hood.

They just stood there, watching me.

"You don't think I mean it? Get out of here." I shooed them with my hands but they still weren't moving.

"Eh, Kinau," someone finally said. I turned to the voice, my fists tight. I was ready for anything. I was already seeing that red dot of blood.

"Try get off my truck, okay?" the man said softly, motioning towards his hood.

That was all it took. I fired into the air and the crowd scattered faster than money. Some ran down the pier, others darted behind trucks and boats, and a few people just stepped away.

"It's over!" I yelled.

A few people nodded.

"Okay, then," I said, as if we'd all come to an agreement.

"Anyone killing another shark has to deal with this." I held the gun up in the air.

The haole cop was moving tentatively towards me, his hands at his sides. The harbormaster was right behind him, his hands explaining, and I heard him say that of course I had a permit.

I jumped off the hood and then Alapai was suddenly there. I threw myself against him, and he held on to me and motioned the cop away and I heard trucks starting up and leaving and when I looked, the fishermen had disappeared off the pier.

"Good, okay," Alapai said, stroking my hair, trying to calm me down. "That was good."

31

I made myself a scotch on the rocks, drank it right down, and made another. I drank half of it while I pulled out a box of bullets and loaded the gun that for some reason hadn't been confiscated from me down at the harbor, and I wondered what I was doing, but not for too long, and I went out onto the lanai and sat down with the loaded gun and the drink. I wasn't sure why I still had the gun with me. My mother had taught me to shoot and probably taught me when to call it quits but I must not have been listening to that part. Still, it felt good to be sitting with a drink and a gun across my knees.

The wind picked up further, and the ti leaves slapped against the house, like someone tapping to get in, but there was no one trying to get in, even though my mother always said that when it stormed in Volcano, the wind shook the ghosts loose from under the eaves of the houses and they knocked to get in, and you should be ready to go with them, at any time. They bathed in the rain barrels, she used to say.

When I finally let myself go ahead and think about Ivan, my desire for him somehow got mixed together with that day in Volcano with my mother, when we picked the white ginger for my father's leis, and I knew I should have gotten rid of him twice. I knew I hadn't taken him far enough out of my life, because when I thought of Ivan I started seeing that dog again, foaming at the mouth, dragging its broken-down body closer and closer, and I thought maybe that's how love looked to me.

After the scotch, I thought how he hadn't exactly made promises to me, but he'd let me believe in a future together, and there was no reason on earth why I should have believed him, but I had.

He hadn't stopped me when I showed how tightly I was bound to him. I touched the gun, felt how rage could change directions when you picked up a gun, could feed down your arms and into the metal itself. It was easy to understand people who said that it just went off.

I went into the kitchen, propped the gun up against the counter, and made another drink. I was dying for something, anything, to step out of the shadows so I could shoot the hell out of it, but nothing did. Besides, my own memory had betrayed me more than Ivan himself. Not even Ivan could have lived up to the man I'd carried with me all these years. I finished the drink on the dark porch with the gun still in my lap. Sometimes even my own life felt like an intruder.

If I shot everything that moved, what would I have left? How many bullets would it take to clean out an ordinary life? I lifted the gun and sighted what was around me. A tangle of strawberry guava trees, a fenceline running downhill behind the greenhouses. 'Ohi'a lehua trees that held still when I pointed the gun at them, shook when my back was turned.

There were two things I figured out while I sat holding the gun. The first was that Ivan believed he had to keep himself moving, the way some sharks had to continuously move, but at the same time he wanted to have everything around him completely still.

The second thing was that I was in love with something that had long since disappeared, and I was the only one who still wanted to believe in it. Even Ivan knew it was gone. Perhaps he'd known it from the start.

When I heard the truck turning off the road and saw the one headlight looking up into the trees, the other straight ahead, I turned off the small porch light. Where the driveway curved he slowed down and I heard glass breaking on the pile of rocks at the side of the driveway. Tossing a bottle.

I picked up the gun, sighted just in front of the headlights, and fired.

The truck slowed down but didn't stop, and I fired again.

Then it stopped and he left the headlights on. The door opened and slammed shut.

"What the hell's going on?" he yelled.

I didn't answer.

"Who the hell is that? Kinau?" he said in disbelief.

"Kinau?" I mimicked. I was capable of that now, I thought, surprised at myself, at how good it felt.

He came around to the front of the truck, in full view. A clear target.

Then it finally hit me, what he'd been doing all along. He wanted to find a way out of his life, the empty life he was too much of a chickenshit to leave.

I wasn't going to be the one to help him. Not me. I was close to shooting, so close that my hands shook, but I realized it was what he hoped I'd do, and I wouldn't do it if that was what he wanted.

I thought about the plans I'd made for our future and I aimed about a yard in front of his feet and fired again.

He jumped but then came a step further. That should have meant something to me, but it didn't. The Ivan I wanted had moved to the Mainland. This Ivan was altogether someone else.

I went back into the house and slammed the door, heard the truck turn around in a spray of gravel and roar off down the hill, and I set the gun down.

He'd leave the way he did the first time, I thought, with just a moment's warning. He'd be holding the rich hand of his wife as the plane carried them higher and higher, away from Hilo Bay, which would twist once and then lie still, and then away from the whole Hamakua coast and then higher, away from Kilauea Volcano, and the plane would bank over Mauna Loa and Mauna Kea and then the island would start to shrink, the way everything always did with Ivan, getting smaller and smaller until the colors ran together and he could believe there was just one shade of green, one shape to the green island squatting like a frog in the shallow water, and the plane moving away until the island became just a smear, a dot.

32

*I*n the next days all the sharks came down, and the fishermen started pulling their boats out of the water and onto trailers. There was a small line of cars and trucks leaving town. People put away their cameras.

The sidewalks were scrubbed down, and Hilo got back its usual look of sleeping in the daytime. But I knew Hilo was swarming with ghosts and now there was one more, and when I walked downtown, it still felt like the sharks were there, still hanging under the eaves of the buildings.

I hiked along the road next to the new lava flow

in Kalapana. It was all new land under my feet, and I got a charge out of it, and at the same time, I thought of the hot springs down at Isaac Hale that were now covered in lava.

When I came to the police barricade, I looked around for cops, as though they had the time and money to sit out here in Kalapana, maybe hide behind some crumbling pile of a'a lava, pounce on all trespassers stupid enough to hike out over the hot lava.

I ducked under the yellow police ribbon. There were kapu signs everywhere, but who were they trying to keep out? The place was deserted. As I looked around I fingered the piece of lava that Ivan had sent to me by messenger from his hotel. One lava flow had gone right across the middle of the road and in the very center there was a crumbly pile of a'a as tall as a house. I climbed to the top and looked over. The new lava flow stretched all the way down to the coastline, right over the cliffs and down into the water. Where the lava hit the ocean, steam was rising like a huge cloud.

I was wearing rubber zoris that stuck slightly to the hot surface lava. As I hiked closer to the shoreline, I heard the lava hiss as it heaved over the edge and fell down into the water. Bits of pumice flew back up, and steam shot up into the air for miles. It was a good place to be, and I threw the piece of lava as far towards the water as I could. When the steam cleared, I thought I saw an old woman standing on the edge of the cliff, right where the lava was pouring down into the ocean. I kept looking at her, saw a telephoto lens in her hands, and laughed at myself to think it was Pele, with a camera.

But then I thought, why not?

What would Pele make of everything that's happened?

It was growing dark now, and I was only a few feet above a rushing stream of lava. I could have put my arm down into it, it was that close, and it was scaring the hell out of me. All I was standing on was a thin crust, while everywhere beneath me, the molten lava was flowing faster than I could run, rushing towards the coast.

I was too scared to move, and then I was running across the lava, jumping from mound to mound. The more scared I felt the more exhilarated I became, and I thought how passion is like a leaping fish, all the wet colors flashing in the sun. We don't give a thought to the larger fish that is chasing it, forcing that beautiful leap.

There are times when the world twists itself into a mirror. In it is the town of Hilo, the scalding lava, the dead boys and the shark-men, the lovers who leave and keep on leaving. The world promises that soon enough we'll even see ourselves in that mirror. Until then, where we need to be is underwater, with one eye on the beast that keeps us moving.